Golden Cloud

PALOMINO OF SUNSET HILL

By **LELAND SILLIMAN**

Illustrated by Pers Crowell

SCHOLASTIC BOOK SERVICES

NEW YORK • TORONTO • LONDON • AUCKLAND • SYDNEY • TOKYO

For Florence, Lynne, and Ronny

Copyright, 1950, by the John C. Winston Company. All rights reserved. This TAB edition is published by arrangement with the John C. Winston Company. Published 1960 by Scholastic Book Services.

5th printing................January 1974

Printed in the U. S. A.

CONTENTS

Other Books by Leland Silliman

THE SCRAPPER

THE DAREDEVIL

THE PURPLE TIDE

1. Homeless

THE light buckboard shivered as it struck a rough spot in the highway, jouncing the driver and the boy who sat next to him. Under different circumstances the excitement of riding behind a horse in this unfamiliar region would have kept the boy straining for each new sensation. But even now, when his teeth jarred together and he slid sideways on the hard seat, the serious expression in Orrin Toler's dark eyes did not change.

It wasn't that Orrin suddenly wished that he had stayed in Detroit instead of traveling to Oklahoma. He knew he would never go back to live with his uncle. If he did not get the job at Sunset Hill Ranch—well, he was nearly seventeen years old, he could take that too. There were other ranches in Oklahoma. But if he had no luck this time, maybe he would drop a line to Uncle Chauncey and tell him about his trip down. He wanted to tell somebody about the things he had already seen, the oil wells in people's front yards, the great wheat fields—

"What's eating you, Bub?" the driver asked.

Orrin made no reply. The man's flat voice lost itself in the squeak and rattle of the buckboard, the creak of harness, the *clot-clomp* of hoofs. Although Orrin's thoughts were not concerned with his surroundings, his gaze took in the details of the countryside. He saw the thin growth of trees bordering a live brook, the green field of Kafir corn in the bottom land, and the freshly harrowed hillside that sloped reddish-brown in the distance, fitting into the pattern like a curved fragment of Indian pottery. He was aware of all this, just as he knew, somewhere far back in his mind, that the driver had spoken.

With a quick movement of his head and a blink, Orrin drove the stare from his eyes and looked at the driver. "Sorry, I didn't hear what you said."

The driver flicked his whip at a horsefly that swooped toward the gray gelding's sweaty rump. "Running away from home, aren't you?"

Orrin's back stiffened. "No!" he exclaimed. "I'm looking for a job."

"Sure 'nough?" the man drawled with a quizzical grin. "I'll be hunting for a job, too, come tomorrow evening. Matter of fact, I wouldn't have picked you up back yonder if I was fixing to stay with Old Man Caldwell. Old Bill counts the number of oats he feeds his horses, and he figures that two can't ride as cheap as one." He chuckled dryly. "If he wasn't so downright stingy, I'd be riding in a Ford instead of this derned buckboard."

"Is that the way folks are around here?" Orrin asked with evident disappointment. "I better get down and walk."

The driver laid his hand on Orrin's knee. "Y'all take it

2

easy. I got a brother up Abilene, Kansas way, and I'll be drifting along to help him ride herd on his wheat fields." Then he added with a friendly wink, "Only reason I mentioned getting fired by Bill Caldwell was so you wouldn't feel ashamed of running away."

"I'm not running away," Orrin said shortly. He half opened his mouth to say something more but changed his mind.

At the boy's reluctance to speak, the driver chuckled and grew very deliberate over examining the smooth leather reins.

Orrin hesitated while he took quick glimpses at the driver's deeply tanned face. There was honesty in the lines around the man's eyes and mouth and friendliness in his manner. Orrin felt a driving impulse to talk about himself and ease the feeling of uncertainty that he could not shake off.

"Maybe I am running away—I'm not sure." Orrin laughed abruptly. "Sounds kind of crazy, I guess, because Uncle Chauncey knew I was going."

"There are different kinds of running away," the driver said.

Orrin gave him a grateful look. "That's right. Most people wouldn't get it."

The gelding's *clot-clomp* gradually slowed as the grade continued upward.

"Living with Uncle Chauncey wasn't doing either of us any good. He's a smooth salesman, but he has just about no use for anybody except himself. While I was still going to high school, I didn't see him so much. But I graduated at mid-term and went to work for him. It seemed like a good idea at the time, because I'll need money if I decide to go to college later on."

"The job didn't pan out, eh?"

"No, except that I made enough money to get down

3

here. After I worked with Uncle Chauncey for about a month, his ways really began to get me . . . Maybe he does have the right slant on the rest of the world. I don't know . . ."

"There's one good way to find out," the driver chuckled. "And if you don't like the answer, I reckon you can always go back."

"Sure." There was no enthusiasm in Orrin's voice. "It isn't as if I had no home at all."

"You never know," the driver said cheerfully. "Perhaps you'll want to stay here once you get located. Can't be that everybody is as mean as Old Man Caldwell."

At this remark the moodiness left Orrin's face momentarily as if a light had suddenly brushed across it. His eyes darkened again; when he spoke there was a mixture of eagerness and perplexity in his voice.

"Do you think that a fellow who likes horses, but who hasn't been around them much, could get by on a ranch?"

The driver looked first at the boy's intent dark eyes, passed over the wide mouth and strong chin, and let his glance follow the full length of the wiry body down to the stout shoes. "Say a lad of about seventeen with Injun-black hair and a look of git-up-and-git about him?"

Orrin watched the driver's face intently.

"If he wasn't afraid of hard work, I wouldn't be surprised a-tall. Ranching around these parts could mean digging postholes or painting sheds. Still, there are ranches—and ranches."

"Do you know about Sunset Hill Ranch?" The question followed quickly.

The driver raised his eyebrows and looked at Orrin more thoughtfully. "Hm-m, now that's a spotted pony of a different color. Sunset Hill is Blacky Martin's ranch, and I reckon he knows just about everything about horses . . ."

The inside of Orrin's stomach seemed to harden, and he slumped back in silence. The driver's manner, as well as his words, brought back all the old misgivings and strengthened them with more real meaning than before.

The gelding's steady plodding had brought the buckboard to the crest of a long, low hill where the land reached out in every direction in broad cultivated fields or great stretches of grasslands. The appearance of a single small cluster of farm buildings, leaning against raw poles, only emphasized the vastness of the space about him. But Orrin caught his breath and continued argumentatively, as if striving more to convince himself than his companion.

"If you want to try hard enough to do a thing, you can," the boy said. "I've found that out. That's how I made the wrestling team at school, and I got so I was selling almost as many vacuum cleaners as Uncle Chauncey."

"Won't do any harm to talk to Blacky," the driver said amiably. "Maybe you can make a deal. You're a high-spirited young colt. However, even the high-spirited ones get homesick, so you won't have to feel bad if he turns you down."

"It'll have to be pretty bad to make me feel homesick."

The driver pulled at the reins, and the gelding, whose pace had suddenly grown brisker, dropped unwillingly to a walk. "See how it is?" the man said. "Even old Dusty know he's getting near home, and it's all I can do to hold him."

"I won't go back to Detroit," Orrin said. "I don't like cities. If Mr. Martin won't take me—" He looked away and his eyes lowered partly from the sun's glare and partly from sudden, overwhelming doubt. But he looked up quickly and went on, "If Mr. Martin won't take me, I'll try again."

"Sounds like maybe you've tried before," the driver reflected as he pulled up the buckboard at the side of the road. "Caldwell's is right around the next bend. You've got a half-mile walk to Sunset Hill. Next place on the right. You'll see the mailbox out by the highway."

Orrin jumped down and thanked the driver, who, with a cheerful "Good luck," slackened the reins and let the impatient gray go *clot-a-clomping* off toward his stall. For a moment Orrin watched and, remembering what the man had said about going home, wondered if he envied the horse.

Several cars whirled past the boy as he walked, but he made no effort to thumb a ride. In a way, he was in no hurry to reach Sunset Hill. A little delay would permit him to take another look inside his thin wallet; allow him time to summon new determination to talk to Blacky Martin of Sunset Hill Ranch.

Gradually his strides lengthened. Mr. Martin definitely wanted a boy. Other places where he had looked wanted grown men. Like that Double Bar outfit where he had heard about the job at Sunset Hill Ranch. This time he would not let himself be brushed off. One thing he had learned in house-to-house canvassing with Uncle Chauncey was not to be bell-shy. And yet, if Blacky Martin knew all there was to know about horses, how much would his helper have to know?

Past Caldwell's place, on along a weedy cotton field, then a pasture, and Orrin could see a mailbox on the right.

"Don't lose your nerve now; this is the best lead you've had," Orrin told himself as he turned up a red-rutted driveway that led to Sunset Hill Ranch. He gave a determined hitch to his belt and headed up the slight grade, his footsteps cushioned by the layer of powdery soil between the ruts.

At the top of the knoll he came to a square white house. Downhill at his right squatted a weather-beaten barn with a fenced-in barnyard that reached all the way to the drive. The rest of the ranch, the pastures, the other outbuildings, the trees and the paddock all fused into one hazy composite picture in which separate details were not distinguishable. He hesitated, undecided whether to hunt through the barn or go back to the house.

While the boy waited, a sudden rush and hubbub from behind the barn caught his ear. Around the corner of the building and headed for higher ground spurted a dodging, bawling red calf. Close behind thudded a cow pony, carrying a rider in a faded plaid shirt who swung a lasso and yelled as he whirled it.

Every thrust of the pony's hard-driving legs brought him closer to the calf. Suddenly the calf, as if realizing the uselessness of his efforts, doubled back toward the barn, almost somersaulting downhill in his haste to dive through a side door.

Orrin's eyes shone under their prominent black brows. This was it! He watched the pony sit back on his haunches, stopping on a dime as the rider reined in and leaped off to bar the door behind the calf.

In an instant Orrin had slipped the wire loop that held the gate and was hurrying toward the barn.

"Is this Sunset Hill Ranch?" Orrin asked the man who had chased the calf.

"Sure is, son." The speaker was slightly bow-legged, and shorter than Orrin by half a head. A few indistinct slants of gray started at his temples and lost themselves in coarse black hair.

The man turned to pat his horse's shoulder and throw

a gruff word into an alert ear. He reached back with his other hand to make a pretense of tucking the tail of his shirt under the waistband of his levis.

"I am Orrin Toler, and I'm looking for Mr. Blacky Martin," Orrin said.

"You've found him, son."

At the twinkle and dry tone of voice, the determined set to the boy's face gave way to a smile that passed quickly, leaving the same earnest expression as before. "I heard that you needed help on your ranch."

Blacky Martin gave Orrin a different look now, a more penetrating one. "You know about horses?"

"I'm crazy about them," Orrin cried.

Martin threw the reins over his pony's neck, slapped a fly that was glued out of reach of the swishing tail. He looked at Orrin and seemed to be estimating the strength in the lad's wiry build. "You're used to hard work. You've got a pair of hands like a bulldogger's."

Martin's statement was so positive that Orrin hesitated to explain that the strength in his hands had been developed by wrestling and working on the wrist machine at school rather than by outdoor labor. But the man was not waiting for any statement. He spoke to Orrin crisply:

"Come on down to the stable, hear?"

The ranchman slid back the big main door, and the heavy fragrance from tier after tier of baled hay rolled out to meet them.

"I call this a stable, but it's more like a hay barn," Martin was saying. "I have only three horses left—that buckskin yonder, a sorrel out in the pasture and my mare." He added regretfully, "Most of my time's going into the dairy now."

"Oh, I see." Orrin's disappointment was so pronounced

8

that he did not notice how Martin's voice had softened in speaking of the mare.

They squeezed between the wall of baled hay and a dusty red tractor. In the rear Blacky Martin swung back a slatted door and the two entered a passageway that ran along an addition to the barn. It smelled more like a stable in here, and a mouse scooting across the wooden floor told of spilled grain near by.

"Here she is," Blacky Martin announced, pride evident in every line of his small, leathery face. He paused before a box stall and looked through the upper half of a Dutch door. "Isn't she a pretty thing?"

Orrin caught a glimpse of pale gold and flowing silver, a slim head with clear eyes and dainty ears that pricked forward. He felt a little breathless, as if he had stumbled into the presence of royalty. "She is a beauty!" he exclaimed. "Pure gold all over except for white mane and tail."

"And four white stockings," Martin corrected. His voice continued softly, "You never saw prettier head nor sounder bone . . . How high would you reckon she stands?"

Orrin floundered. "Oh, she must be about—well, I'd say she was a pretty good size."

"Sixteen and one," Martin said with a sharp glance at Orrin, "and the smartest hunter you've ever seen. Three-quarters thoroughbred and mated to a palomino stallion with Arabian blood. She'll drop her foal later this month. And, son, just between the two of us, I'm spending all my spare time hoping that it'll be another palomino like its ma."

"Well, why wouldn't it be—" Orrin began, and then stopped suddenly, so as not to reveal his ignorance about palominos. To cover the unfinished sentence he

9

became interested in peering through a knothole into the next stall.

Blacky Martin took a slow, shrewd look at Orrin—this boy with the quiet, self-reliant appearance of a ranch-bred lad and a tongue that had stumbled twice in talking about horses.

The mare's sleek head was reaching farther and farther through the opening, while her soft lips nuzzled at the pocket of Blacky's plaid shirt. Mechanically the ranchman's hand slid out a lump of sugar toward her as he scolded her. "Just like a spoiled child. That's what you are." He fondled the smooth muzzle and pulled affectionately at her silver forelock.

Orrin had edged closer as Martin talked, and now his hand reached toward the gleam of the mare's neck. His fingers stroked the hair, soft and lustrous to his touch.

"There's a loose nail on that board yonder," Blacky Martin said with concern. "I'll slip into the stall and pull it out before Queen nicks herself." He drew a pair of pliers from a pocket of his levis.

Eagerly Orrin seized the pliers before Blacky realized what the boy was doing. Orrin unbarred the door, pushed against the mare's flank with a confident hand. "Over, Queen, that's the lady," he urged in a firm voice.

The boy seemed utterly at home with the horse, so sure, yet so gentle in his motions. Suddenly Blacky's eyes sparked with a warning; Orrin could hear the swift intake of breath as the rancher cried:

"You're on her off side, boy. Watch out!"

There was a clatter of hoofs and an angry snort as the mare whirled in the stall.

Orrin started to jump back, but Blacky appeared beside him, and shoved the boy toward the door. At almost the same instant he leaped for the mare's head.

10

The crack of Queen's hoofs resounded against the stall like gunfire as Orrin slipped through the door.

While Blacky crooned the mare back to normal, Orrin waited outside, trying not to breathe heavily after his narrow escape. "Her off side," Orrin thought bitterly. "Something tells me I'm still looking for a job."

He was trying hard to regain a confident air when Blacky stepped out of the stall and said shortly, "You can't make mistakes with Queen; she's one high-strung lady." Blacky Martin leaned over a wisp of hay and carefully chose a short stem. Chewing it and frowning at the same time, he strolled back to the main part of the barn. Behind him, Orrin shortened his steps and looked unhappily at the back of the rancher's neck, where the black hair had been cut in a straight, unwavering line. Until he had gone into the stall, Orrin had dared to hope that he was making a favorable impression on Blacky Martin. But now . . . well, there was no use thinking up excuses.

Outside the barn the buckskin pony was nodding sleepy-eyed. Blacky paused by the mount, fingered the smooth russet of the saddle, and finally turned and said bluntly, "You don't know much about horses."

"No, sir," Orrin said weakly. He thought miserably of Uncle Chauncey's slick patter and compared it with his own clumsiness now. Maybe if he took his uncle's advice and looked down on everybody as a sucker, he would do better.

Blacky muttered something and looked at the boy's hands. "You still look like you can do a day's work," he said with a certain doggedness as if reluctant to change his original impression of the boy. "That's as much as you can say about anybody nowadays. I can use you for maybe a few weeks if Clara is satisfied. Come along."

In silence they climbed the slope of the barnyard,

crossed the drive, and stepped up to the back porch. While the two soberly scraped their shoes, Orrin, feeling a little more self-confident now, braced himself for the meeting. Mrs. Martin would be a big-boned, aggressive woman. Little men always married that kind.

A minute later Orrin was standing inside the kitchen, facing a small woman in a man's blue work shirt and a plain gray cotton skirt. He reached out awkwardly to shake her left hand.

"I caught it in an ensilage cutter when I was a child," Mrs. Martin said simply, with a nod toward the stump of her right hand.

"Oh—I see," Orrin said through his surprise at finding Mrs. Martin so tiny and pleasant. He would have added that he was sorry about her hand; but there was a quality of sweetness in Mrs. Martin's gray eyes and a competence about her manner that made Orrin feel sure she would not care for sympathy.

"I think I was born to be left-handed anyway," Mrs. Martin smiled. "Shall we go to the living room?"

Blacky Martin waited until his wife was seated before he pulled up a pair of straight-backed chairs for himself and Orrin.

The living room was square, a cheerful room with a beamed ceiling. But Orrin's attention was particularly attracted to the pictures on the walls. Every one had to do with horses. He sat down opposite a colorful rodeo scene that was amazing in its reality.

"Taking a little ride out into the country?" Mrs. Martin prompted.

Orrin looked away from the picture and glanced toward Blacky, but he could read nothing in the blank, brown eyes. Blacky's was the sort of expression that a quiet man wears in church. The assertiveness that he had shown outdoors had disappeared here in his wife's presence.

Orrin replied slowly: "Yes, Mrs. Martin, I took a little trip out here for a special purpose. I want to work on the ranch."

The words did not displease Blacky's wife. At least her smile lost none of its pleasantness. "We have a fine dairy," she said. "It is going to be the best one in Oklahoma some day. But I didn't know we were looking for help."

Blacky Martin spoke now, looking humbly at his wife from a slight angle. "We really need a boy with the horses. I'm hog-tied to the dairy a smart of the time, and we can't take chances with Queen—she being nearly ready to drop her foal. It would pay us to take on a boy just to watch her." He sounded like a man who eyes a luxury and tries to convince himself that it is a necessity.

"Isn't Gabe going to do any work this time either?" Clara Martin asked.

Blacky's reply sounded a trifle vague. "You can't depend too much on Gabe. He might not get here for another two, three weeks. And then he'll be busy trading around for breeding stock. You see, Orrin could help out around the cattle too."

"He won't get near the cattle if you have your way," Mrs. Martin said briskly. She turned to Orrin. "If you go to work for Blacky Martin, he'll want you to groom Queen all day and sleep in her stall nights."

"I'd like that!" he cried. "I'll make friends with Queen fast enough. I've never seen a horse like her."

"You and Blacky sound like two of a kind," Mrs. Martin declared. "Do you go around with your shirttail hanging out all the time too?"

In spite of her words there was something warm in

Mrs. Martin's expression that made Orrin hope she had taken a liking to him. While Blacky in embarrassment hurried to tuck in the tail of his shirt, Orrin replied meekly, "No, ma'am."

"Then I expect it would be right shameful to refuse you the job. The east bedroom is ready to move into today."

"You won't be sorry," Orrin said. "Mom had a lot of Cherokee blood in her, and I'll take to horses the way she did. I know I will." He clasped his hands around one knee to hide the excited quiver in his fingers.

"That might be, and then again it might not," Blacky said. His shrewdness seemed to be returning now that Clara had given her consent. "We haven't talked wages yet. I'll pay you twelve-fifty a week with room and board—until Gabe comes."

"You'll give him fifteen," Mrs. Martin stated promptly.

"Fifteen," Blacky repeated obediently.

Orrin was off his chair in an instant, a smile broadening his naturally wide mouth. "I'll be back early in the morning," he said, backing toward the kitchen door. "I left my things at a rooming house—and thanks a lot for the job!"

As the boy hurried toward the driveway, his thoughts began to straighten out. Blacky isn't too crazy about me, and I guess there are better guys to work for. But Queen! Mm-m-m, what a horse! And Mrs. Martin sure is one swell person.

The more he reflected, the more excited he became. The driveway was gold dust that his feet scarcely brushed. "It can't be true," he thought excitedly. "I've got a job on a real ranch. All I've got to do now is make friends with Queen. If Blacky will let me alone, I'll do that in nothing flat—I hope."

For a moment the thought disturbed him that the person called Gabe might appear soon to end his job. Then, measuring the distance back to the little square ranch house, he raised his voice, which would remain under control no longer. "Yippee! Ride 'em, cowboy!"

2. Sunset Hill Ranch

THE dew sparkle and eagerness of early morning covered Sunset Hill when Orrin Toler returned the following day. He responded to its cheerful effects the moment the truckman with whom he had ridden rumbled out of hearing. Under its charm he felt more certain than ever that he had made no mistake in running away from Uncle Chauncey's influence, even if this Sunset Hill job was not steady. He stood with his suitcase beside him at the edge of the road, content for a time to stare at his long shadow that leaned against the road. He grinned as he thought how pleased and surprised he had been by Mrs. Martin's hospitality; and he tried to catch again in his imagination the extraordinary beauty of Queen, the palomino mare.

The thud of hoofbeats fitted so naturally into his

thoughts that at first he paid no attention to their increasing sound. It was only when the tempo dropped sharply away that he jerked his head around and started at the reality of two figures drawing up their horses.

Before he could slide things back into focus, he heard a girl laughing at him. "You looked awfully silly just standing there."

Now Orrin caught an impression of a girl's face bent along her horse's neck—a homely face with a pair of impudent, wide brown eyes under the brim of a derby hat. In her neatly pressed riding clothes she might have come directly from a show ring.

"I thought you were a statue," she said. "Can you talk?"

The question was asked with such pert directness that Orrin retorted, "Don't you think you better ride home and tend to the milking?"

The girl laughed again. "I finished milking half an hour ago."

"We've got milking machines," a small boy's voice added proudly. "Don't mind what Barbara says. You visiting around here?"

The boy's brown hair needed cutting, and his features were somewhat sharper than the girl's, but it was obvious the two were sister and brother. The boy's mended jacket and dungarees contrasted oddly with the girl's outfit, but Orrin liked his alert, inquisitive face and the ease with which he sat bareback on his tall bay.

"I didn't mind what Barbara said," Orrin replied stiffly. A glance up at her showed that she was still amused, and Orrin, feeling his annoyance return, spoke directly to the boy, "I've got a job at Sunset Hill Ranch."

"Poor thing," Barbara commented as she deftly reined her spirited mount in a narrow circle.

"Why?" Orrin demanded.

"They've been getting rid of all their horses. Besides, there's Blacky's cousin Gabe. He's supposed to be working in Texas, but he's around here half the time. He won't stand for anybody else living at the ranch."

"We'll see about that," Orrin said shortly.

The girl looked surprised. "Has Blacky stopped supporting him?"

Orrin realized that he could not back up his words, that he knew practically nothing about Sunset Hill Ranch. But the girl irritated him, and he tried to hold his position. "Don't be too sure of yourself. There might be a few things you don't know."

"Sounds fishy to me," Barbara said, looking hard at Orrin. "I bet you can't even ride a horse. Here, I'll get down and let you try Spice."

Orrin pressed his lips together and reached for his suitcase.

"See you riding around," Barbara laughed. "We're neighbors. Come on, Tad, I'll race you down to Caldwell's." The words merged into a clatter of hoofbeats and she was off, but Tad did not join her. Instead, he swung his leg over the bay and slid to the ground.

"Barbara's stuck up since she's been going away to school," he confided, "but she always was ornery when she was on a horse. Inside the house or working around the place she acts different. I feel kind of sorry for her sometimes."

"She sure knows how to ride," Orrin muttered as he stepped closer to pat the boy's horse.

"It's all Sis cares about," Tad said. "She hardly talks to anybody unless he's a good rider. Hey, are you really going to help Blacky keep his horses?"

Orrin hesitated, ashamed to tell the truth to a boy. At last he said awkwardly, "Well, I guess I was doing some loud talking, but you don't have to tell your sister. Besides—" and now he was not speaking impulsively as he had to Barbara, but with a thoughtful frown— "besides, something might turn up to change things."

Tad looked at Orrin with more respect. "I hope so. Blacky used to have a slick string of horses. Reckon I'll be going now."

Orrin looked at the big horse and then at little Tad. "Want a boost?"

"Not me," Tad cried. After withdrawing a short distance he made a running jump for the horse's back. In some amazing way he scrambled aloft while the animal patiently endured the tugging at his mane and the prodding of sharp little knees. "Made it the first time," Tad panted as he gathered up the reins. "Well, so long."

Orrin admired the unstudied skill of the boy as he rode off; but frowned because he himself had missed the opportunity to grow up with a horse under him. "I'll make up for lost time," he promised himself. "Maybe I'll even be fit to ride with Barbara some day, if I get so I can stand her."

As Orrin lifted his suitcase, it felt heavier than it had before. The talk with Barbara and Tad had driven away the dreamy satisfaction that had been with him earlier. He eyed the near-by acres of Sunset Hill Ranch critically. What yesterday had blended into an indistinct aura of corrals and bunkhouses and lush pastures now stood revealed for what it really was. The rail fence at his right was unpainted, and broken in places. The dairy buildings were hidden beyond the knoll; and as for bunkhouses and cowboys, there just weren't any.

However, as he walked, Orrin's moodiness gradually decreased, and he realized that the ranch was not altogether run down. A grove of pecan trees at his left was vigorous and well spaced. The Bermuda grass pasture beyond the rail fence was dotted with shade trees, protected against grazing animals by triangular rail guards. From one of the near-by branches a bird sang to the early March sunshine.

"A mocking bird," Orrin thought, not really knowing or caring if he was right, but pleased by the bright song. He shifted his heavy suitcase to his left hand and watched his long shadow stride ahead of him to the back door of the ranch house.

A knock at the door brought no response; the house had a hollow sound. He opened the door and started to push his suitcase inside, hesitating long enough to rub the dust off it with his hand before sliding it onto the gleaming linoleum. Then he started toward the barn.

Blacky Martin was not in sight when Orrin reached the barn, but the tractor was standing outside, smelling of freshly burned gasoline.

"Mr. Martin!" Orrin called through a crack in the big sliding door.

The muffled whinny of a horse was the only reply. Orrin slid the door open far enough to slip through. A continuous whinnying and whistling reached him now, clearer inside. As the boy swung back the slatted door in the rear, the dust from the hay tickled his nostrils and made him sneeze. The voice brought a frenzied outburst from the mare.

The top half of the door to the stall was closed now, but he could catch glimpses of the palomino moving about impatiently between her trumpetlike calls.

The mare's cries sounded so insistent that Orrin began to wonder if she were in pain. "Maybe the foal is coming," he muttered. He took a tentative look behind him, uncertain whether to search for Blacky or to stay here.

"Easy, girl," he soothed her. "There, now. Everything is all right." Realizing that he would have to make friends with Queen before he could do the job for which he had been hired, he reached into the stall in an attempt to give the mare a pat, but she shied away from it. Her tramping sounded louder than ever as the minutes passed.

Orrin's mind was made up now. He hurried back to the door and reached it at the same moment that Blacky Martin got there from the opposite direction.

"I was looking for you—" Orrin began without even a hello or a good morning.

"Were you now?" Martin interrupted. "Could you wait long enough for me to feed Queen? I'm fifteen minutes late this morning, and she's calling me down for it."

"Oh!" Orrin's tense expression shaded into embarrassment, which Martin was too busy to notice.

"Here's the tack room," Blacky said with a curt nod of his head. "You'll find a clean bucket inside. Go right through to the paddock and fill it up with water from the trough under the windmill."

Orrin replied with a quick, "Yes, sir," relieved that his first chore was one he could do without asking questions.

He picked up the bucket, but stopped long enough to draw in a slow breath. The tack room overflowed with the smell of leather and neat's-foot oil, and Orrin liked it. In passing, he slid his fingers over a saddle that hung on a peg, as he had seen Blacky Martin do the day before. It felt good, and he allowed his finger tips to linger on it for a moment. Then he hastened out to find the watering trough.

When he returned to the mare's stall, Blacky was pouring a measure of grain into a metal trough in a far corner.

"Back already?" Blacky grunted as he straightened. "Here, let me have that water." He removed a pail from a shelf in the corner opposite the feedbox and swung the fresh water up in its place. "Now you can clean this bucket and leave it in the tack room for next time." He paused long enough to note the T-shirt that Orrin was wearing, with a black TEAM across the chest. "Athlete, eh?" he commented as he put a halter on the mare.

Orrin nodded, but made no reply. He doubted that a ranchman would be impressed to know that he had been captain of the wrestling team at his high school back in Detroit.

Blacky Martin's voice was impersonal as he gave Orrin his final instructions before hurrying out. "I have to get to the fields with the tractor right quick," he said. "After Queen finishes eating, lead her out into the paddock and clean the stall. There's plenty of clean straw in the back of the barn. When that's done, give her a good grooming; you'll find everything in the tack room."

Orrin looked perplexedly after Blacky's busy little figure, thinking all the while of his narrow escape yesterday from Queen's hoofs.

Blacky paused at the end of the passageway. "Had your breakfast?"

"No, but that's all right, Mr. Martin," Orrin replied, his mind struggling with the difficulties involved in carrying out Martin's orders.

"You go to the house now," Blacky said. "Clara is back from the cow barn, and she'll fix you up with a good meal. Go right away, hear?" And Blacky was off.

Clara Martin was in the kitchen, pouring milk from a shiny pail into two-quart containers. She had seen Orrin coming and had opened the door for him. As he stopped to wipe his feet, Mrs. Martin nodded with approval. "Next time you come in, don't knock," she smiled. "You're one of the family, and we're proud to have you." She held up a bottle for him to see. "Good rich Jersey milk.

I'm putting an extra two quarts in the refrigerator for you."

Orrin gave her a grateful look. It had been a long time since his needs had received such kindly consideration. He watched Mrs. Martin pour out the rest of the sudsy milk, marveling at the deft way she used her crippled right hand.

"You'll want to wash up," Mrs. Martin was saying. "The bathroom is off the southwest end of the living room. Use the towel that hangs over the tub."

Orrin's dark face was shiny and his black hair in rebellious order when he returned. He carefully closed the door to the living room, sealing the smell of fried bacon in its rightful place, for he had noticed that Mrs. Martin had closed it after him when he went to wash his hands.

There were toast and canned peaches on the kitchen table and a pile of bacon that almost hid two fried eggs.

"We have cereal too. Would you like some?"

The size of the breakfast overwhelmed Orrin. "You've gone to too much trouble, Mrs. Martin. I'll never finish all this."

"Nonsense." Mrs. Martin added a tall glass of cold milk to the battery of dishes that faced him.

Orrin ate in thoughtful silence while Mrs. Martin hustled about the house. It was surprising how the breakfast disappeared. Maybe it was the change from cafeteria eating, he reflected.

"There, see, you've done it," Mrs. Martin said as she started to clear off the table.

Orrin was on his feet at once to help her. "Let me wash them."

"You have the mare to look after," Mrs. Martin teased. "You ought to be out in the stable grooming her now.

Who knows—there might be a speck of dust on her somewhere."

"May I please help you?" Orrin pleaded with a grin, feeling pleasantly at ease with Mrs. Martin.

Clara Martin gave in with a pretended warning. "Don't let Blacky catch you washing dishes when a horse needs attention, or he'll sure fire you."

Orrin's mind was on grooming horses as he splashed the soapy water over the dishes. He looked quickly toward Mrs. Martin once or twice, almost started to speak, but thought better of it. "I'll do a better job of salesmanship today," he thought. He pretended to be making conversation as he said, "Mrs. Martin, did you ever groom a horse?"

"Hundreds of times."

"Did you ever try cleaning them without a currycomb?"

Mrs. Martin paused to give the boy a searching look, but there was a guileless expression on his face. "Maybe just to slick them up . . . No, you've got to use a currycomb—" She broke off suddenly and looked closely at Orrin. This time his eyes dropped, but he was certain that Mrs. Martin was not angry.

"If you want to know how to groom a horse, why don't you come right out and ask?" she demanded, but a twinkle showed in her gray eyes.

Orrin's resolution not to give in and admit his ignorance vanished. "I didn't want Mr. Martin to find out how little I know about horses," he confessed. "I've got to prove that he didn't make a mistake in hiring me."

Mrs. Martin did not hesitate. "You're clean and honest and willing to work, that's what matters. Now, suppose this ironing board is the mare. You'll start on her near side like this, dandy brush in your left hand and curry-

24

comb in your right . . ." Mrs. Martin moved about the ironing board while Orrin followed every action.

"Thanks a lot," he said when the demonstration was over. He was thinking about more than the lesson in grooming. Strange, but he felt more at home here already than he ever had with Uncle Chauncey.

Mrs. Martin went on, "Now, if you want to make a special hit with Blacky, wad up a handful of straw and polish Queen with it after you finish with the rub rag." Her thumb flicked off the lid of a metal canister, and she held out two lumps of sugar. "Too much of this isn't good for her, but you'll find it will come in handy to make friends. She'll be skittish at first. Let her get used to having you around before you make up to her. Land sakes! I can leave this ironing long enough to see you get started right."

"No," Orrin said quickly. "I'm not going to begin my job that way. You've helped me plenty." He hung the towel on the rack and, pausing momentarily, gave Mrs. Martin an impulsive pat on the shoulder as he left.

Mrs. Martin watched the boy's lean figure disappear up the drive. "Something's been bothering him for a long while," she mused. "He doesn't smile enough. But he's a willing boy, and smart too—the scalawag—wanting to know if I ever tried grooming a horse without a currycomb!"

But her thoughts quickly gave way to concern. "I shouldn't have let him go out there alone. Queen has a sharp pair of heels."

3. The Foal Is Born

BACK at the stable Orrin and Queen appraised each
other across the top of the door. The mare was
quieter now, but her eye held an uneasy gleam. Her
stamping made the planks vibrate under Orrin's feet as
he looked for a lead rope.

He worked deliberately, careful to follow Mrs. Martin's advice and not offend the mare. At first he moved
casually just outside the stall, where she could become
used to seeing and smelling him. Then he rested his
forearms on the door and held one lump of sugar on
the flat of his palm with his fingers stretched out of the
way of Queen's teeth. The palomino's fine ears pricked
forward, while Orrin talked to her quietly. He felt a
warmth inside him as Queen stretched her muzzle toward his hand. After a moment's indecision she ad-

vanced a step and reached for the first lump of sugar. Orrin held his breath while she daintily lifted it from his palm.

The brush of soft lips on his hand seemed like an invitation to enter the stall, but he had learned caution yesterday and decided to wait for a while.

"Now," he said softly to himself after another half-hour spent near the stable door, "let's see what happens." The next few minutes would be risky. Should Queen turn on him with teeth and hoofs, the result could be fatal. Orrin's careful movements showed he was aware of this. He knew that Blacky Martin was not standing by to help this time, that he was entirely on his own.

Holding the other lump of sugar so that Queen could see it, Orrin unbarred the door, and with a tingle that started in his chest and crept up to his throat, he stepped to the mare's near side. Her ears flattened, and she backed away a half-step.

Orrin realized his danger, but he was not afraid. It seemed natural for him to be here. His pulse beat quickened, but there was exhilaration in its throb. He would win Queen's confidence all by himself. His words rang with quiet power. It was as if his mother were speaking through him. "Quiet now . . . Easy . . . Here's another lump of sugar."

After a tense moment, Queen's love of sugar overcame her distrust, and before she had time to change her mind Orrin had snapped the lead rope to her halter. "Outside with you now," he ordered, and threw open the door to the paddock.

The sunshine sought the rich coat of the mare as she swung through the door, and slid about in gleaming high lights as she moved.

Following Mrs. Martin's directions, Orrin tied Queen

to a rail behind the stable. He worked over the mare for a long time with hands that calmed as they polished the warm gold of her body. He smiled to himself with satisfaction.

When Blacky came down for the tractor, he took a few precious minutes to duck into the paddock. To Orrin's relief he was pleased with Queen's appearance, chuckling as he played with her.

The boy heard Blacky say to the mare, "It *is* going to be another palomino, isn't it, old girl?"

To Orrin, Blacky commented, "I'll be harrowing yonder in the west fields. Let down the bars to the pasture for Queen. Then you can finish cleaning out the stall and set things aside in the barn. You'll hear Clara ring the bell when it's time for dinner."

He whistled as he hurried about his duties. He would clean the stable as it had never been cleaned before. One impelling thought pushed all others from his mind; this was the kind of place where he could really be happy. Then he got to thinking uneasily about Blacky's cousin Gabe, and his whistling stopped. He tried to tell himself it made no difference, that his own job would last but a few weeks anyway. The important thing was that he belonged to ranch life and not to Uncle Chauncey's narrow, self-centered world.

The stall was neat and clean when he finished, with the pleasant odor of fresh, dry straw crowding out the stable smell. By the time Clara Martin rang the dinner bell, Orrin had straightened out the tack room and swept every bit of bare floor that he could find. Two large blisters were swelling on his palms, and his shoulders and back were tired from the hard work, but he would toughen up fast. It had been only a few months since he had been working out on the wrestling mats two hours a day.

Dinner was served in the kitchen. Blacky Martin said grace and then fell quickly to eating so he might hurry back to the fields.

"What do you want me to do this afternoon?" Orrin asked before Blacky had finished his broad wedge of apple pie.

"You're all caught up? Tomorrow I'd like you to run the tractor while I take the pickup to Oklahoma City. This afternoon, well, the horses need riding. Pick one out and take a look around the ranch. The worst dude in the world can ride my horses. They'll take you where you want to go even if you were to sit on them backward."

It seemed to Orrin that this reference to his lack of experience could have been omitted, but the unexpected opportunity to ride on his first day made him forget his blisters and sore muscles. He looked hopefully toward Mrs. Martin, who gave him a reassuring smile. He then turned to Blacky, "Thanks a lot," he said. "I'll take you up on that."

"Take the sorrel," Mrs. Martin advised Orrin after her husband had gone. "She's gentle and gaited; used to belong to a retired gentleman up Tulsa way."

"Can you give me an idea how to saddle her?"

"I'll go with you," Mrs. Martin replied. "I can't show you on the ironing board this time. Here, I'll take a few pieces of carrot with me."

On the way to the barn Orrin said in a puzzled voice, "Mr. Martin seems awful afraid that Queen's foal won't be a palomino."

"You can't tell about palominos," Mrs. Martin explained. "They don't always breed true to type. Then, too, there's the chance that a foal will be born with a glass eye. There's a breeder near Dallas who will pay a fancy price for a sound palomino out of Queen." She caught her breath. "Yes, Blacky and I are both hoping awfully hard."

He lugged a saddle out of the barn while Mrs. Martin carried a saddle pad and the bridle. At the pasture fence she whistled and held out the pieces of carrot, and presently a reddish horse came ambling up.

"Ripple is hackamore broke," Mrs. Martin explained as she slipped the bridle over the horse's head with her good left hand. "The bridle doesn't have any bit, but she's gentle as a rocking-horse."

Orrin studied Mrs. Martin's moves closely and then heaved the saddle up on top of the pad. Mrs. Martin showed how tight to pull the girth, then lengthened the stirrups for Orrin's long legs. "Hold the reins like this in your left hand, and work them against her neck."

"Ready?" Orrin asked eagerly.

"Yes. Put your left foot in the stirrup—turn it around this-away. Grab the saddle horn. There, now swing up into the saddle."

The horse stood quietly except for stamping a fore-foot, perhaps to discourage a fly.

"Where's a good place to ride?" he asked, excitement edging his voice as he searched the countryside.

"Anywhere you want to, but you better keep away from Caldwell's place yonder. They have an ugly dog that gets loose sometimes. You could ride west toward the Canadian River. Our land runs a long way in that direction. But the riding gets bad unless you keep to the lane at the end of the driveway." She held the gate while Orrin guided the sorrel out of the pasture. "Good luck," she called, with a wave of her hand as he walked the horse up the drive.

Beyond the barn the drive curved around the side of the pasture where Ripple had been grazing. From farther to the north and west, the whine of Blacky's tractor came faintly against the steady south wind. Soon the pasture gave way to bottom land and Orrin could look across a broad field of alfalfa to where Blacky rode his machine.

When the drive rounded the western borders of the tilled fields, Orrin turned Ripple into the lane that Mrs. Martin had told him about. Tall weeds and grass, thick with sand burrs, pushed against what was little more than a trail. Here and there a deep erosion gully, like a raw, red gash, drew his attention. Too bad so much land was cut up like this.

This was the first time he had ever ridden off alone on a horse. It sent his thoughts back to early childhood before his family had gone to China, where his parents had died of a strange fever. Back to the exciting times when his mother used to visit friends on a farm outside Detroit to help exercise the horses. He could see her now, galloping through the meadows, her face darkly elated, glorying in the speed and rhythm of the sport. And little Orrin, dark like his part-Indian mother, would listen to the throb of the hoofs and swell to the thought that he would soon be big enough to ride all alone too. Then his mother would lift him to a saddle that was much too broad for him and laugh at him for kicking vigorously at the horse's sides.

Orrin patted Ripple's neck and frowned. His uncle had been as contemptuous of horses as he was of people. Except for a pony ride now and then, Orrin's experiences with horses had come to an abrupt end.

The memory of his mother's swift gallops suddenly made Orrin rebel at barely crawling along. Ahead, the trail stretched weedy but level, varied occasionally by an outcropping of flat, red rock. He dug his heels into the sorrel's flanks. Ripple broke into her slow gait, as gentle for the rider as sitting in a club chair.

"There's nothing to riding," Orrin exulted. "And to listen to that snooty Barbara, you'd think you had to be practically a genius." He looked ahead of him with confidence.

"That's a funny place for a truck cab to be," he muttered to himself. Ahead of him, a powerful cab rocked over the trail at slow cruising speed. He could see the two men inside, who kept turning their necks in every direction . . .

"Probably lost," he thought. He urged his mount on faster so he could catch up with them.

The result was a fast trot, with Orrin bouncing about in the saddle like a ball caught between crosscurrents. His respect for Barbara's riding ability suddenly returned, and he risked a fall to look back to make sure nobody was watching him.

In spite of his discomfort, he refused to pull the horse back to a walk. On he lurched, clutching at the saddle horn and twisting himself in all sorts of positions. His heels must have kicked Ripple's sides, for suddenly she surged into a full canter.

Orrin's head jerked back for a moment, and his first impulse was to yank on the reins, but he fought for balance, and to his surprise the jouncing stopped; suddenly he became part of the horse. Ripple must have been anxious for a good run, for she stretched onward with no urging. Or perhaps she sensed the sharp pleasure that the rider felt in having her gallop this way.

Before Ripple's burst of speed closed the distance between Orrin and the two truckmen, a jet of exhaust spurted from the cab, and Orrin heard the roar of its motor above the pounding of Ripple's hoofs.

"Nice of them to get out of my way," he thought, "but what's their hurry?"

There was a limit to how far one should ride a horse

hard. He did not know just what that limit was, but he did not want to injure Ripple, so he regretfully reined her in. For a time the boy's body had synchronized with the swift pace of the ride; his quick breathing still reflected his mood. So far ranch life was even better than he had dreamed!

As Ripple continued at a walk, Orrin watched for the truck cab without success. Queer how it had kept going ahead into nowhere. And where was the truck that it should have been attached to? He decided he had better tell Blacky about it.

He walked the sorrel all the way back. As he drew closer to the ranch house, he found himself twisting and squirming in the saddle in an effort to find a way of shielding the chafed spots on his legs.

To his surprise, Mrs. Martin was down near the barn mending a hole in the pasture wire with a pair of pliers and a coil of wire. She stopped when he appeared. "Have a good ride?" she asked.

Orrin's face gowed in spite of the soreness that was making the saddle seem like an invention more fiendish than anything used during the Inquisition. "A swell ride, Mrs. Martin!"

Together they rubbed down the sorrel as they talked. "Did you get to put her through her paces?"

"We had a little gallop," Orrin replied. "I don't know what else she did, but I do know it just about shook my teeth out."

"Sure 'nough," Mrs. Martin laughed. "You must have had her at a trot. There's a little secret about trotting that I'll tell you about some other time."

Supper was late that evening so that Blacky could use every possible minute in the fields. When he stepped into the kitchen, his first question was to his wife: "You fed the mare?"

At her reassuring nod, Blacky's mood improved. He turned to Orrin. "Some day after the foal is born, you'll want to take a bit of lunch and ride all the way to the river . . . There are doves there in the fall." His voice concluded on a lower note, and he looked toward his wife out of the corner of his eye.

Mrs. Martin, who seemed to be paying no attention to either her husband or Orrin, commented placidly, "And there's fourteen head of grade Jerseys in the south pasture, counting heifers."

Orrin let a moment pass and then brought up the question that was in his mind. "Did you happen to see two men riding ahead of me in a truck cab this afternoon?"

Blacky turned swiftly and raised his eyelids. There was a pause and then his brief chuckle. "Probably a couple of hunters getting the jump on the season."

After supper, when Mrs. Martin had stepped out to the milkhouse, Blacky found the previous day's *Oklahoman*. He folded back the pages and pointed to a small item.

Orrin read the article twice, gravely. Thieves operating from trucks had been rustling stock in northern Texas. He did not like the sound of it. A vivid picture of two men craning their necks in the cab of a truck stood out in his mind.

"No use to worry Clara," Blacky said curtly. "Nobody's going to mess with scrub Jerseys." He added under his breath, "I sure wish, though, we could watch Queen better at night."

Orrin heard him. "I'll sleep in the stable," he offered. "I meant it when I said so before."

"You couldn't do that—Clara would never stand for it if I asked her." Blacky put just the subtlest emphasis on the word *I*.

Orrin surmised what Blacky meant. "Want me to ask her?"

Blacky's attention seemed concentrated on the pattern in the wallpaper, and he addressed his reply to the opposite end of the room. "Well, she sure seems to put a lot of stock in what you say."

"I'll ask her then."

To Blacky's obvious surprise, Mrs. Martin agreed, although she insisted that they set up a steel cot in the barn for Orrin to sleep on. Personally she selected the right spot to place it, for as she remarked, "It's still March for all the hot weather we've had, and this barn is a right drafty old place. Over here behind this straw you'll be snug—and close enough to Queen to hear her if she gets acting up. Goodness knows we can't afford to lose the money a good foal will bring."

Later, when Blacky and Orrin were together in the barn, the rancher handed him a flash light. "Check up every hour or so. No use to light up the whole barn."

"Sounds like a good idea." Excitement blurred Orrin's words together.

"Now I'll watch my chance when Clara's busy and fetch you my shotgun." Blacky's heels clicked against the barn floor and then the sound was muffled and lost as he went out.

"I'll load this and leave it on safety," Martin said when he had brought back a single-barreled shotgun. "But use it only as a last resort. Here, throw these into your pocket too." Blacky dropped two more shells into Orrin's hand as he left, but again reminded him to use the gun only in an emergency.

After Blacky had gone, Orrin sat on the edge of the cot with all the lights out and alert to catch every sound under the broad roof. The scuffle of a mouse in a far corner, the creak of a timber contracting in the evening's cool, the rasp of a cricket.

Before lying down, he tiptoed to Queen's stall, walking in the circle of light from his lowered flash light. He knew that there was no likelihood of the foal's being born yet, although Blacky had let Clara think it might be. Neither did it seem possible that thieves could steal the mare from the stable even if they knew about her. Still, like Blacky, Orrin wanted to take no chances with Queen.

With his ear against the stall, he listened in the darkness until he heard the mare stir; he felt the floor shake underfoot as she shifted her weight. Satisfied, he slipped back to his cot and fell asleep.

Throughout the night he slept fitfully, and consequently, he had no difficulty in making regular trips to the stable. Once he heard a thumping noise from outside the barn that brought a crawling sensation to the back of his neck. But investigation from the back door of the tack room revealed nothing more than Blacky's buckskin pony wandering near the paddock fence.

It must have been about four o'clock in the morning when the noise of a distant explosion came faintly to Orrin's ears. It might have been a shot fired by an early rising poacher, or it might have been a truck's back-firing! He picked up the gun and hurried out to the paddock, keeping the flash light turned off.

Orrin waited tensely in the heavy shadow of the barn, the tip of one finger resting on the safety of the gun. As his eyes became used to the darkness, he could see the buckskin pony in a far corner of the paddock, asleep standing up.

The tension in his chest that made his breath come in shallow drags was beginning to wear off when a darker shadow behind the rail fence made him fully alert again.

The shape of a man's head and shoulders was silhouetted momentarily above the fence. Before Orrin could force himself to call out, the man had vaulted the fence into the paddock and was heading directly toward the boy.

Orrin's lips parted to challenge the trespasser, but a sudden idea held him silent. Although he had the gun, he could not fire point-blank at a man. The fellow was not burly—better to seize him in a pinning hold and yell for Blacky.

Orrin dropped the shotgun and charged when the stranger was about twenty-five feet away from him. He had always been an aggressive wrestler at school, but never had he been keyed up in friendly competition the way he was tonight. The man's amazed grunt ended in a pained *oof* as Orrin's head hit his stomach and a pair of long arms wrapped around his legs, throwing him violently to the ground. The impact jarred Orrin too, and he fumbled as his hands groped for the man's neck and shoulders.

In that moment of hesitation, the trespasser squirmed and pitched suddenly. Catching the boy a fraction off balance, he gained his feet. Orrin lunged for a new grip, but the darkness aided the man, who tore away with a final wrench, dashed for the fence, and scrambled over it. Orrin leaped after the fleeing shadow for a few swift strides before he remembered the shotgun.

By the time Orrin had found the gun, further pursuit was useless. He scowled down at the weapon while he sputtered at himself for being so clumsy. "I suppose Blacky Martin will be real pleased when he hears about this," he muttered savagely. The catch of the truck's starter and a blast from its motor took Orrin's attention to the cornfields. From beyond a grassy hill a pair of headlights flashed as the truck circled over the rough ground toward the highway.

Orrin ran toward the house, which rose silent and unnaturally large in the grayness preceding dawn. It was not going to be easy to make his report. Uneasily he began to reason with himself. "Maybe it would be smarter not to say anything to Blacky. He's going to get sore because I didn't catch that guy . . . might even want to fire me . . ."

He frowned at the square ranch house. "I'm only sticking my neck out if I tell him . . ." But these thoughts did not slow his long strides. Other ranches would be in danger, and perhaps Blacky could send out the alarm. Orrin ran lightly up the back steps and stole upstairs.

"Mr. Martin, Mr. Martin," he called softly at the bedroom door so as not to wake Mrs. Martin if he could help it. If she should answer instead, he would have to do some fast thinking.

"Mr. Martin—"

Someone was sliding out of bed. "That you, Orrin?" came Blacky's sleepy whisper as the door opened. Then, as he stepped into the hall, his low voice demanded tersely, "What's happened?"

"The guy in the truck cab," Orrin whispered. "He got away."

"You saw him?"

"Yes, but—"

"I shouldn't have depended on a kid," Blacky growled. "I'll throw a couple of blankets in the barn tonight and sleep there myself."

Warm blood flushed Orrin's cheeks. "You won't have to do that," he declared. "I won't let them get away the next time."

"All I can do now is to run over to Johnson's and call the police," Blacky muttered as he returned to the bedroom; and Orrin, feeling the impact of the boss's anger, wandered back to the stable to talk to Queen.

Later in the morning Blacky found an excuse to postpone his trip to Oklahoma City, but the day passed quietly. When night came, he made no move to sleep in the barn, but he warned Orrin that nothing must happen to Queen.

All night he stayed grimly at his post, brooding because Blacky thought he had not lived up to his trust. It would be too bad for anybody who prowled around the stable tonight. But nothing happened before morning, and after another tense day and night Blacky told Orrin that the thieves had been caught heading west through the Panhandle of Texas. Nevertheless, the rancher ordered Orrin not to get lax, in case there were others roaming the country.

In the week that followed, he learned a great deal. At times he helped around the dairy, climbing to the bottom of the sour-smelling pit silo near the cow barn and forking out the ensilage while Blacky worked the hoist above, or hosing down the floors in the barn while the cows were at pasture. Twice he spent the day in the broad seat of the tractor, riding endlessly back and forth, with all the world screened off by the clamor of the engine.

A few evenings later Blacky spoke to Orrin after a trip to the stable, and there was excitement to his voice. "Keep a close eye on Queen tonight. If she starts to walk around kind of nervous and breaks out in a sweat, come get me."

Orrin caught the note in Blacky's voice. He lay awake for a while wondering about the foal, hoping it would be a palomino. Finally, with a last long breath of hay-scented air, he rolled over and slept. In an hour's time he shook himself, reached for the flash light and tiptoed to the stall. Everything was all right, Queen was on her side sleeping.

At intervals all night Orrin made his inspections. At three o'clock he thought he heard the slow thud of hoofs. He stared above the baled hay into the deeper shadow of the mow and listened. There it was again! The tips of his fingers tingled as they closed on the flash light.

In the narrow beam of light, Queen moved about uneasily, her flank showing the dark stain of perspiration.

"Get going," Orrin told himself, the urge of excitement quickening his thoughts and actions. His swift footsteps sounded lightly in the passageway as he ran for Blacky.

Into Blacky's bedroom window Orrin shot the rays of the flash light, and immediately the ranchman's head appeared. He waved and disappeared, slipping outside a moment later and buttoning his shirt under his open jacket as he came.

"There are two clean milk pails in the kitchen," Blacky barked as he hastened off to look at Queen. "Fill them with warm water and bring them to the stable."

Orrin, following a few minutes later with a pail of water in each hand, ran head on into Blacky at the open barn door. Even in the darkness Orrin knew that the ranchman was worried.

"We'll need a vet," Blacky snapped at once. "Queen's in trouble."

"No!" Orrin gasped. It had never occurred to him that the splendid mare herself might be in danger at the birth of the foal.

Blacky was pulling roughly at Orrin's arm, leading him back toward the driveway and talking at the same time. "Take the pickup and go fetch Doc Rawlings. The first hundred and sixty beyond the crossroads—about eight miles south. You'll know it by the big sheep shed with a new tin roof."

"Keys in the pickup?" he asked, and broke into a run.

"Yes," Blacky called, dropping behind now. "And don't

let Doc put you off. He gets ornery spells, but he's the best vet with horses this side of Forth Worth. Don't dare to come back without him, hear?"

Orrin's foot pushed hard on the accelerator as he skidded out on the highway and headed south. A lumbering milk truck swayed over to the side of the road in response to an insistent *beep-beep*, and the driver looked out curiously at a lean young figure bending behind the wheel of a careening pickup.

Over and over in the course of the ride, flash backs of the mare came to Orrin. He could feel the soft nudge of her lips on his hand as she lifted a bit of carrot or apple; he could hear her shrill command to be fed when he was late with her breakfast. He squeezed another five miles an hour from the vibrating machine. "She's *got* to be all right," he said aloud. He remembered Queen's eyes, soft and alert, but fearless. "She's got to be."

There was no mistaking Doc Rawlings' place, with the metal roof of the sheep shed catching a faint gleam from the stars. The high-pitched roar of the motor dropped quickly as the pickup rattled into the vet's driveway.

Orrin leaped to the porch and rapped on the door. There was no response. He took a few quick, impatient steps on the porch and knocked more sharply. Could it be his luck to find nobody at home? Finally a light shone through an upstairs window. "Who is it?" a sleepy voice grumbled through the window screen.

"I'm from Blacky Martin's place," Orrin called back.

Some more grumbling from upstairs, while his temperature rose hotly because of the time he was wasting.

A light appeared in the living room; a tall, gaunt man with a face seamed like an old leather traveling bag pushed open the front door. He had pulled on a pair of

41

gray trousers, but he still wore a striped pajama top. "What is it?" he demanded roughly.

"Blacky's palomino mare is having trouble with her foal," Orrin cried. "Can you come right away?"

"I'm too sick to go anywhere," came the sour reply, and Doc Rawlings banged the door shut.

Orrin was anxious to raise himself in Blacky's opinion, but more important, Queen was desperately in need of a vet. Without hesitation Orrin jumped forward and opened the door. "You've got to come!" he insisted. "You couldn't let anything happen to Queen."

"Why not?" Doc Rawlings snapped. His thumb reached for the light switch.

"For one thing, you have the reputation of being the best vet this side of Forth Worth." Orrin stood in the frame of light looking up pleadingly at the vet. He thought wildly of dragging Doc Rawlings along bodily if he refused to come.

"A-a-ah," Doc Rawlings growled. "I probably have pneumonia right now . . . What was that you said, the best *what* this side of Forth Worth? Don't try to flatter me, young fellow."

"I'm only telling you what I heard." Orrin caught a trace of weakening in the other's voice. "Doctor Rawlings, please come. You know Queen!"

Doc Rawlings made no intelligible reply, but he snatched a coat from the back of a chair, pulled it over the pajama top, and fumbled on the floor of a closet for his veterinarian's bag.

Orrin slammed the pickup door behind Doc Rawlings and jumped on the starter before the doctor could have a chance to change his mind.

The vehicle shot into Sunset Hill Ranch with Doc Rawlings holding the seat with his left hand and the door handle with his right. "I'll *walk* back," he muttered as he climbed to safety.

"Come on," Orrin cried. "Blacky's down there in Queen's stall."

Perspiration had plastered a lock of Blacky's hair across his forehead, and his face was taut, but he managed to mutter to Doc Rawlings, "There's still a chance, Doc . . . Whatever happens to the foal, you've got to bring Queen through alive."

Doc Rawlings only grunted. He was on the job now, the best vet with horses short of Fort Worth, and his mind was on his business.

A shakiness struck at Orrin's knees as he inhaled a long, grateful breath, but the job was not yet finished. For the next hour or so, he hurried swiftly about at Doc Rawlings' bidding. The world was the inside of a huge bowl, blue-black except for the gleam of Orrin's flash light as he ran back and forth to the house, and the flood of light in a stall where Blacky and the doctor knelt at Queen's side.

Daylight was dulling the glare of the electric lights when Doc Rawlings peeled off his rubber gloves and called for Orrin. He came on the run, but stopped short just inside the stall. There was Blacky smiling down at a long-legged creature with soft, sleepy eyes lying on a rubberized sheet next to the mare.

The boy blinked at the damp, ruffled hide of the foal and began to grin.

"Spunky little devil, isn't she?" Blacky asked proudly as the foal struggled to rise on wobbly legs. "Queen sure did herself proud, son—with Doc Rawlings' good help—and I sure thank him. There's as pretty a little palomino filly as you'll ever see!"

Doc Rawlings added gruffly in Blacky Martin's direction, "You might thank the boy, too, Martin. He did what was mighty near the impossible. I'd made up my mind I wasn't going *anywhere* last night; but, so help me, he plumb changed my mind."

4. What Price for the Filly?

AFTER Orrin had returned from taking Doc Rawlings
home, he hung around the stable with Blacky
Martin for another half-hour, feeling an inner flow of
excitement that increased each time he came close to
the foal. The wonder of seeing the soft-eyed creature so
full of life and beauty, and yet so dependent, fascinated
him.

As soon as a light brightened the kitchen window,
Blacky ran to the house to bring Clara down to the
stable.

"She's beautiful; she's sure a pretty creature," Mrs.
Martin breathed. "Oh, Blacky, she has the four white
stockings you wanted!"

Blacky hovered about proudly, chuckling as if it were
a surprise that he had known about from the beginning.

"Now I reckon I can go back and get some sleep," he said with satisfaction when they had all exhausted their exclamations. "And, Orrin, you needn't show up until tomorrow morning."

But Orrin felt no drag of fatigue. This new experience reached far beneath the surface of his thoughts, deep inside where dreams begin. It tugged at him with a strange insistence that he made no attempt to understand; he only knew that he must give in to a driving desire to remain alone near the filly. "I'll be up a little later," he said, hiding his feelings with an offhand manner.

"You're the boss," Blacky grinned as he walked away with Clara.

Orrin puttered about the stable, humming to himself or talking to the filly who, after a little, seemed to accept him without fear. He completely forgot about breakfast until Clara rang the bell from the back porch.

"Better catch some rest while it's still cool," Mrs. Martin advised after Orrin had swallowed a quick meal.

"Maybe later," he replied, and ran back to the stable.

During the morning the filly took a few shaky steps in the big box stall. Orrin, realizing that he was the first person to see her walk, felt a new thrill. He praised her, and laughed when her long ears twitched as if to catch the words.

After lunch he tried to rest, but he had hardly stretched out on his bed when he thought of an excuse to pull his shoes back on and slip out to the stable. This time the filly permitted Orrin to stroke her, although she stayed close to Queen, who made attentive, motherly sounds.

Increasingly, as Orrin watched her every movement, the filly emerged more and more as an individual. The way she tilted her fine muzzle when she heard a noise,

46

the twitch of her delicate nostrils, the clean flow of lines in her short, golden body, the swish of her little white brush of a tail. There had never been so beautiful, so lovable a young animal, of that he was certain. He was filled with thoughts that struggled for expression, but there was no one to talk to. His mother would have understood. Maybe Mrs. Martin would too, but he did not know her well enough to confide in her.

It was past midafternoon when Orrin heard someone open the barn door and a strange voice call inside. Jealously he stood at the door to the box stall and listened. Somebody was calling his name. He walked back to the slatted door and asked gruffly, "Who is it?"

"May I come in? I mean, do you mind?" It was a girl's voice, timid.

"Oh, hello," Orrin said, casually, but hardly civil as he recognized Barbara in an old black felt hat with the strings tied under her chin.

"Blacky said it would be all right," Barbara ventured, appearing as awkward on foot as she had been graceful on horseback. No matter what she did with her hands, her elbows stuck out like grasshoppers' knees. "Could I see her? My spring vacation ends tomorrow and this is my only chance."

"Come on," Orrin replied. He stalked ahead and threw open the top of the door to the box stall.

"O-o-oh!" Barbara exclaimed with a depth of admiration that took Orrin by surprise. For a long while, that was all she said, nothing sarcastic, not even the flip re-remark that he had expected. She just stood there, lithe and natural, her brown eyes seeming to widen and shine.

"Will she let you—?" Barbara whispered.

"Go in there?" Orrin asked. "Watch me."

To him it seemed one of the proudest moments in

his life. Barbara certainly appreciated the unusual beauty of the filly. On that basis he accepted her as a friend for the time being. But Barbara did not know all the filly's little tricks and mannerisms. Only Orrin was familiar with these, and he was the only one the filly would trust in the stall. He remained in the stall for a few minutes, stroking the fuzzy, golden hair, and talking to Queen as he petted her foal. Barbara watched him with shining eyes.

"Jeepers, you're lucky!" Barbara exclaimed when Orrin rejoined her. He just looked at the filly and smiled.

"Well," Barbara said, glancing around and sticking out her elbows at uneven angles, "I think I'll go now."

Orrin remembered that Tad had spoken about feeling sorry for his sister at times, and now he understood what the youngster had meant. "Come again," he invited her.

"Maybe when I get back for the summer," Barbara replied. She walked away, stumbled self-consciously, and exclaimed at herself for being clumsy.

"Queer kid," Orrin thought as she hurried out of sight, "but she knows horses." He wondered about her for a minute and then forgot everything else except the filly.

For the next two days, except for a casual visit from Tad and Blacky's regular inspections, Orrin had the stable to himself. When the foal was in her fourth day, two men from Anadarko stopped to talk to Mr. Martin. Orrin had just finished feeding Queen when Blacky brought them in to look at the filly.

Blacky acted good-natured but wary with the men. "Open it up," he told Orrin, pointing to the top half of the door. "These fellows want to look inside." Orrin moved slowly to obey. There was a studied indifference in the manner of the visitors that told him they were here for just one purpose—to bargain for the filly if they liked her.

If they liked her! Orrin caught the quick, greedy look in the stouter man's eyes when he saw her. The filly, seeing strangers, slipped nimbly behind the mare before they had a chance to study her.

Queen stood tense, with ears laid back, and rolled her eyes at the stout man.

Orrin watched the visitor stumble back a step. "Easy now," he coaxed, purposely standing so that the strangers could see nothing but his back and part of Queen's neck.

The stout man had recovered his air of indifference. He removed his flat-crowned hat and rolled the brim in his hands. "Reckon she's just an ordinary filly," he drawled. "Step out the way, son."

Orrin obeyed slowly and the men pushed closer.

The mare's sleek head turned vigilantly, and the filly faded around to put Queen's body between her and the enemy.

Orrin stood back on tiptoes, keeping an eye on the alert foal, while he listened to the conversation.

"What are you asking for her?"

Orrin's fingers gripped the edge of the open door as Blacky gave a short chuckle. "To tell the truth, I'm not fixing to sell her yet," Blacky said.

Orrin's hands eased off the door. He walked away a few steps, but returned when he finally heard the two men saying, "So long."

With a last snort Queen turned to her foal, nuzzling her anxiously. Orrin glanced concernedly at the filly's close-coupled, golden body and saw that she was no longer frightened. He stepped in to give Queen a pat, and turned to find Blacky at his side.

The rancher's eyes were dark with excitement. His hands made quick moves to his hips, to his jacket pockets. "That heavy-set fellow just made me an offer of eight hundred dollars for the filly—"

In silence Orrin frowned, and his eyes studied the filly from her thin baby head to her scrubby white tail.

"—and I turned him down."

After Blacky left, Orrin stood with his fingers twined in the filly's mane and stared at the corner of the stall. "I hope Blacky doesn't get his price until after I leave Sunset Hill Ranch," he thought.

At the supper table that night Blacky Martin became unusually talkative. "I been thinking," he said to Clara, "the barn would look right pretty with a new roof. Another thing, too, maybe we could get a man to paint the rail fences. They sure would look nice all white and shiny."

Mrs. Martin spoke to the point. "Any loose change we can dig up better go to improving the herd. What we need is a pure-bred bull with a record for producing heavy milkers. We've got to be practical."

The next morning was mild and sunny. Blacky, still in high spirits, told Orrin to turn Queen and the foal into the paddock. Orrin spoke soothingly to the mare and bribed her with a carrot as he led her from the stall. He stood clear of the door while the foal followed her mother into the strange, outdoor world. Then he stood in the doorway and watched the filly crowd close to Queen's side. Through wide eyes, tall ears, and alert nostrils she explored her new surroundings. Cautiously she ventured a few feet away. At the sudden whir of the pickup's starter near by, she jumped behind Queen. The mare reassured her with a nip at her scanty white mane.

The smell of green grass, exciting but without meaning, filled the foal's nostrils. She nuzzled under Queen's stifle for a drink of warm milk.

During the day Orrin kept track of the filly's progress as best he could. Once he saw her separated from Queen by a good thirty feet. Whimsically she kicked up her tiny hoofs and charged back on long legs that held more speed than she knew. He chuckled as the foal galloped ten feet past Queen before she could stop.

In the days that followed, Orrin won the friendship of the filly completely. She recognized his whistle, the sound of his footsteps inside the stable. When Blacky and he appeared together, she would look past the man and tease the boy for the touch of his hard, lean fingers.

At the same time another friendship was developing. One day the filly had been met at the paddock fence by the same red calf that Blacky had once chased on his buckskin. After a brief period of inspection through the rails, the filly pivoted on her slim legs and raced experimentally along the side of the fence. On the other side, the calf took up the chase until they reached the corner of the paddock. Each morning after that the filly would wait at the fence for her playmate. Up and down they would frolic, the filly kicking up her hoofs on one side of the fence, the calf streaking along the other side, its ropelike tail with a little kinky twist in it flying up in the air. But even in the middle of their play, a whistle from Orrin would bring the filly to him on the dead gallop.

There were many visitors during these days—neighboring farmers, curious about the little palomino, shrewd breeders and trainers making poker-faced bids for the striking filly. At each visit Orrin's face would assume a wooden expression, but Blacky continued to hold out. Every chance he could get, he would stop by to play with Queen and talk to the filly. "A foal is just as good as her head and feet," he told Orrin, "but I can't fault this one anywhere."

Hearing him talk this way, Orrin wondered if Blacky had decided not to dispose of the filly after all. But the continued offers for the animal kept Blacky keyed up, and Orrin was afraid that the impulse to make money would force Blacky to sell her.

The excitement over the filly's birth and then the anxiety over her future had almost made Orrin forget about Blacky's cousin Gabe. One day when Orrin stopped at the mailbox, he found a letter bearing a Texas postmark, addressed to Blacky. The writing was large and scrawling, with a blot across the lower corner. A premonition slowed his footsteps as he carried it to the house.

He fidgeted while Blacky thrust a blunt forefinger under the flap of the envelope and pulled out the letter.

The rancher's voice was noncommittal as he remarked to his wife, "Gabe's coming next week."

Clara Martin glanced at Orrin and back to her husband. "I can fix him a bed in the spare room."

During the next few days Orrin attacked his chores with a solemn intensity. If either Blacky or Clara noticed it, neither one mentioned it to the boy. Several times he nearly asked his employer when he would be through at the ranch, but somehow he never quite found enough courage to say it. Every moment that he could spend with the filly now was treasured. He was still devoted to Queen, but his affection for the filly was different, more possessive. He was standing at the open gate to the pasture, watching the beautiful foal kicking her heels about when he decided on a name for her.

"Just like a little golden cloud," he reflected as he watched the filly drift effortlessly over the turf. "That's what I'll call her," and he repeated the words softly, "Golden Cloud."

He whistled and called "Golden Cloud." The filly spun and galloped to the boy, poking her nose inquisitively against his shirt. "Golden Cloud," the boy repeated once more. So far as he was concerned, that was going to be her name.

The filly responded to her name as readily as she answered Orrin's whistle, by the time Gabe Martin arrived from Texas. As it happened, Orrin was prettying up the little palomino the first time he saw Blacky Martin's cousin.

He was burnishing the filly's short, golden back with sweeps of his rub rag and trying to keep her head from bobbing in all directions while he was working on her. Golden Cloud heard the approaching footsteps first, and her ears pricked forward in curiosity.

"Y'all know where Blacky is?" called a drawling voice from the paddock fence.

"Gone after a load of feed." Orrin gave Golden Cloud a final swipe before he looked around.

The resemblance between Gabe and Blacky was noticeable, although Gabe was much bigger and coarser-looking than his cousin. As he slouched against the fence, his elbows resting on the top rail, he appeared to be about twenty-two or twenty-three. A new fawn-colored Stetson sat back on a mop of black hair that had a definite curl. Many people would have thought Gabe handsome.

Gabe whistled at Golden Cloud and grinned as the narrow muzzle swung toward him. "Hello, Tubby," he greeted the filly.

Orrin frowned at Gabe's flip speech and the bold way he stared at her after he saw how perfect she was.

However, Gabe evidently felt quite at home, for he remarked carelessly, "As long as nobody is around I reckon I'll give old Ripple a little exercise. I've got a

53

pair of boots in here somewhere." He shook the traveling bag that he had brought.

"Mrs. Martin is up at the dairy," Orrin said, but Gabe was already strolling toward the house.

There was a hurt look in Orrin's eye as he followed Gabe's self-confident figure. He threw an affectionate arm over Golden Cloud's withers and stared off across the hills. The Martins would not keep both Gabe and himself at the ranch—that he was sure of. The filly's right ear twitched back, and then forward, as if sympathizing with the boy's mood. Suddenly his gaze jerked back to the filly and his eyes grew moody. "Go find the calf and have a good run," he said gruffly, with a slap on Golden Cloud's flank, "I've got my chores to finish."

Orrin was dragging down a bale of straw, and handling it roughly, when Gabe returned.

"Hey, hired man," Gabe cried with an impudent grin, "how about saddling Ripple for me." He stood as tall as Orrin, but he was broader across the shoulders and many pounds heavier.

The patronizing tone Gabe used struck Orrin like the slap of a hand. He realized he was annoyed, but he knew he must not lose his temper.

"Well?" Gabe grinned.

"I'm sorry," Orrin said evenly, "but Mr. Martin told me to hurry up and clean out the stable."

The smile left Gabe's face. "Funny thing you had time to play with that filly yonder."

Orrin attacked the straw without looking up again, but he knew that he had made a bad start with his boss's cousin.

Gabe passed Orrin on the way out without a word. From the corner of his eye he noticed that Gabe carried the heavy saddle as easily as if it were a pillow.

The fellow had given every indication of being spoiled and lazy, but he was definitely a powerful man.

"What's the difference what he's like?" Orrin thought gloomily, kicking the bale of straw. "He's taking over anyway."

Still Orrin could not resist watching through a stall window while Ripple was being saddled. Gabe had his cousin's skill with horses, but lacked Blacky's consideration for animals. Orrin frowned as he saw a bridle with curb bit slide into Ripple's mouth, and in the sunlight he caught the gleam of spurs on Gabe's boots.

Ripple reared under Gabe's rough handling, but the rider wasted no time asserting himself as master, as he headed the sorrel straight for the bars that served as gate. Ripple faltered momentarily, but caught her stride in time to jump the gate nicely. Orrin could not help but envy the young man's horsemanship as he galloped out of sight. He finished his work at the barn and scrubbed for two hours at the milkhouse, and was back at the barn oiling the mowing machine when Gabe clattered right onto the barn floor with Ripple. The mare had been ridden hard: gobs of lather speckled her chest; her heaving sides were soaked with perspiration, and her nostrils flared red.

"She needs more work," Gabe said with a nod to Ripple His eyes shone from his own enjoyment of the ride as he swung to the floor. "Give her a good rubdown." He left before Orrin could refuse.

The sorrel had been walked, rubbed down and watered when Blacky drove up with a load of feed. He called to Orrin, who was leaning over the saddle on the barn floor. "Why didn't you wait until after supper and I'd have gone riding with you."

"Your cousin is here," Orrin said glumly. "You weren't around, so he decided to go for a ride."

Blacky's thick eyebrows lifted. "Did anybody take care of his horse?"

"I did."

Blacky shouldered a bag of feed in silence while Orrin carried saddle and bridle into the tack room. After he had hung up the saddle, he straightened and drew in a long breath. It had been a hot day, his back was tired from continuous work, his arms were streaked with dust and sweat. Any job would seem easy after this. Let Gabe Martin do the work that Orrin had been doing at the ranch and see how he liked it. Mechanically the lad mopped the perspiration from his eyes with his shirt sleeves and went to help Blacky unload the feed.

Most of the talk at the supper table that night was supplied by Gabe Martin, who sounded gay and expansive. He told stories of wrestling steers at rodeos, and life on the endless acres of a Texas ranch with himself the hero of most of the tales.

Blacky listened eagerly, and if Orrin had not felt so depressed he too might have found entertainment in the swashbuckling tales. Once Blacky put a direct question to Gabe, asking him if he would be ready to run the cultivator the next morning. Gabe laughingly replied that he had to look at some brood mares he was thinking of buying.

After supper Gabe said briskly to Mrs. Martin, "Shall I throw my things in the east bedroom, Clara?"

"I made up the bed for you in the spare room this time," Mrs. Martin told him.

"What's the matter with the east room?"

"Orrin is sleeping there."

"Can't he move?" Gabe grunted.

"I reckon he could, but he's not going to." Mrs. Martin looked at him with undisturbed calm.

Orrin could see that Gabe resented her remarks. Hoping to shield her, Orrin offered. "Let me have the spare room. It'll only be for a short time."

Mrs. Martin agreed reluctantly, her gray eyes fixed on Orrin with a troubled expression.

The next morning Orrin went about his duties sluggishly. There had been no opportunity to come to an understanding with the Martins about when his job would end, but it was on the boy's mind. He finished grooming Queen, but wasted no time, and he deliberately suppressed his desire to fondle her. Golden Cloud nuzzled Orrin expectantly, but he spent only a few minutes with her and did not offer the usual tidbit. She cocked her head to one side and seemed to be struggling to understand her part in this new game. Then she tried a few steps, saucily tossing her head and looking back at Orrin, but he was not looking at her.

Finally the puzzled filly trotted away to sniff through the fence at the red calf. Orrin, watching her, drew a slow, heavy breath. He decided to find Blacky and quit immediately.

Blacky, who was seated on the tractor, saw the serious look on Orrin's face and tried to be the first to speak, but the lad blurted out, "I came to tell you I am quitting right away."

"Well, now, I wouldn't be in any such hurry," Blacky drawled.

"You have Gabe," Orrin went on doggedly, "and I'll only be in the way."

Blacky shook his head slowly. "You hang around awhile, son. Gabe isn't ready to go to work yet. Moving around makes a young fellow restless; besides, he's going to take time buying some stock."

Orrin found his determination to leave growing weaker. He knew that the sooner he made the break the better, but thoughts of Golden Cloud, Queen, and Mrs. Martin held him silent.

"You do as I say," Blacky insisted; and the motor in the big red tractor broke into a roar.

As the week passed, he saw little of Gabe, who was usually absent from Sunset Hill Ranch for one reason or another. When the two met, Gabe treated Orrin with good-natured condescension, calling him *hired help* or *hired man*, often to the accompaniment of a clap on the shoulder with a thick hand. All this Orrin took with as good grace as he could, but he was angry with himself for remaining at Sunset Hill.

"Hey, hired help," Gabe called to Orrin one day when they met in the barn, "here's a good exercise to help you work up an appetite for breakfast." He hoisted a full sack of feed on each shoulder and did ten deep-knee bends, heaved the feed back to the floor and laughed, "Try it some time."

Knowing well enough how Gabe liked to show off, Orrin was nevertheless annoyed. He knew he could not perform the feat, and as usual let the incident pass.

Another time Gabe slipped behind Orrin and seized him in a bear hug, pinning the boy's arms to his sides. Gabe gave a pleased laugh. "Y'all reckon I'm still healthy enough to wrestle a steer?" He gave a powerful squeeze and easily swung Orrin off the floor.

This bit of play very nearly rubbed through Orrin's patience. He would gladly have turned and matched his wrestling ability against Gabe's power even in a rough-and-tumble struggle, but he was afraid of the consequences of a brawl and once more put up with Gabe's pranks.

A frown settled on Orrin's face as he watched Gabe stride off, and he muttered to himself, "I wonder how much more I can take before something pops?"

5. The Frontier Club

You've got everything looking slicker than a hound dog's tooth," Blacky told Orrin on Friday afternoon. "Think the filly would miss you if I carried you to Oklahoma City while I attend to some business?" There was a strange eagerness in the rancher's small features.

Orrin had never felt close to Blacky. The gap between expert horseman and novice had always stood between them. But now Blacky sounded so friendly, and Orrin's own thoughts had made him so restless, that he felt particularly pleased with the invitation. Another reflection made him hesitate, however. "No, I guess I better not go. I can help Mrs. Martin if I'm here at milking time."

"Sure 'nough?" Blacky said mildly. "What do you know about that? I've already told Clara you're going, and she said the sooner you got out the better."

"That does it then; I'm going."

As they rattled down the driveway in the pickup, Orrin stuck his head out of the window and looked back toward the house, thinking how much different everything had appeared to him a month ago.

"That rail fence *would* look better with a coat of paint," he remarked.

"We can't paint that and buy a bull too."

Orrin had forgotten that painting the fence was tied up with selling the filly. He added hastily, "I was thinking that maybe I could finish my chores faster and paint a little bit each day."

Blacky glanced at him quizzically. "You're doing a smart of work as it is. I don't know what makes a young fellow like you want to do any more."

Orrin, thinking about the insecurity of his job, tried to force a grin, but failed. "I guess it's because there's a lot of work to be done." He could not tell Blacky that it was because at last he had found a place where he felt at home. He couldn't act like a cry baby and try to explain the lonesome, numb feeling that hit him whenever he thought of leaving Clara Martin and Golden Cloud.

The squeaks and rattles of the pickup were not interrupted again until Orrin asked, "Is this a short cut to Oklahoma City?" He looked suspiciously at the road between the pieces of tape that held the windshield of the old car together.

Blacky's expression was half-smiling, half-sheepish. "We'll get to Oklahoma City all right," he chuckled. "There's a sort of meeting going on out here a few miles farther. We'll just stop by for a minute, so I reckon there's no need to mention it to Clara."

They rode on in silence except for the metallic clatter of the pickup. The smell of last winter's antifreeze boiling off in the radiator killed any fresh spring scents from the countryside. But the trees and bushes were freshly leafed, the wheat fields green and flourishing.

Orrin had no idea what Blacky's destination might be, but he was not surprised when the pickup slued off the highway where an arrow pointed the way to the Frontier Club.

"Nothing special going on at the club today," Blacky observed. "Some of the boys just hanging around, and some training their horses for rodeos. Here we are now."

Over the top of a tight board fence Orrin could see gray plumes of dust rise into the air and then bend into scattered wisps when the breeze caught them. A wide gate in the fence sagged open, allowing Blacky to run the pickup into a crude parking space just outside the wire fence of a country rodeo arena.

"They've got some swell horses here!" he exclaimed. "Boy, look at that chestnut!"

"Russ Ordway's pony." Blacky's eyes looked eagerly past the chestnut with its neatly hogged mane and braided forelock. "They'll start the calf roping presently."

Most of the activity was centered at the other end of the arena, where a platform rose directly above a half-dozen stout-timbered chutes. Some older boys and girls in bright plaid shirts sat on the floor of the platform, their legs dangling over the chutes. Several men slouched inside the arena, smoking cigarettes, joshing one another so that their voices carried to Orrin's ears now and then. At the far end of the inclosure a rider was urging a spotted cow pony into an open chute.

"Joe Fallon," Blacky muttered at Orrin's ear. "He hasn't roped a calf since they opened Cherokee Strip."

Finally the spotted pony was backed into the chute, tensely ready to spring forward. The rider flipped a cord between his teeth, leaned forward with lasso coiled, and nodded to the starter. Somebody jerked open the next gate, and a Brahma calf dashed out. When the hard-running calf had a few yards' lead, the judge snapped open the barrier and the spotted pony broke for the streak of dust kicked up by the Brahma.

Fallon's body was leaning sharply forward now as he whirled his lasso over the pony's head. In an incredibly short time the horse bore down on the calf, and Fallon bent over farther to make his throw. An instant before the rope was released, the calf doubled in the direction of the fence. Angrily the roper stopped swinging the loop as his horse swerved in pursuit.

From then on it was a battle between the horse and the calf, and Orrin missed no detail of the event. The calf had been chased many times before; he knew all the tricks. If he could reach that open gate at the end of the arena before being thrown, he would avoid a mauling. Just as surely, the spotted pony knew that he must keep on the heels of the calf or his master would sear him with sharp leather.

The calf hugged the fence a few yards more, but hearing the swift flurry of hoofs close behind, suddenly shot out into the open. Calf and pony were directly opposite Orrin when Fallon's lasso swooped down, throwing the calf on his side. Immediately the cow pony threw his weight backward, skidding to a stop on his haunches. Fallon leaped out of the saddle and, grabbing the taut rope, ran toward the calf like a swimmer following a life line.

"That calf is sure going to break loose," Blacky muttered. When Fallon was three-fourths of the way down the rope, it happened. The horse was doing his best to keep the rope tight by backing slowly away, but the loop slipped back toward the calf's hindquarters. With a convulsive heave and lunge the calf freed itself and, after limping a few steps, fled into the pen.

Fallon turned to the horse, jerking the rope savagely as if the animal were to blame for the mishap.

"That man has no business owning a horse," Blacky snapped. A ridge of muscle bulged along Blacky's jaw and an explosive-looking light flared in his eyes.

The enraged squeal of a horse drew Orrin's attention from Blacky to the arena, where the spotted pony was rearing on his hind legs and trying to strike back with his forefeet, but Fallon was his master and was punishing him mercilessly with a quirt.

At the first blow, Blacky shouted, "Stop that!" In two swift movements he climbed over the wire fence.

Fallon's quirt was poised for another cruel blow when Blacky snatched it out of his hand.

"Stop! Stop!" he cried.

As the quivering horse sprang away free, Fallon snarled something at Blacky, who immediately drew back his right hand. For a moment Orrin was certain that Blacky would cut at Fallon with the quirt, and Fallon must have feared so too, for he ducked back, throwing his arm up in front of his face as a shield.

But Blacky dropped the leather quirt and struck Fallon across the cheek with the flat of his hand. His head hardly rose above the other's shoulder, but in his anger he seemed to tower above Fallon.

"Now catch that pony and gentle him," Blacky ordered as Fallon backed away uneasily. The rancher stood there until he saw that his command would be followed out. Then he turned and motioned to Orrin to join him by the chutes.

As he hurried along the outside of the fence, Orrin realized that Blacky's action had held up the practice. But now another calf was released, and a rider chased him through the gray dust of the arena, making a neat catch before the calf had run forty yards. The horse stopped nicely but failed to back up. The roper pursued the calf while it plunged at the end of the slack rope. Finally he tripped the calf and lashed its feet with a few turns of rope.

When he reached a gate by the chutes, the same man was patiently making his horse back away, while he pulled back at the end of the lasso. The lesson was conducted firmly, but with consideration for the horse's lack of experience. Blacky grunted his approval this time, but his eyes were still smoldering, as he said to Orrin:

"That spotted pony yonder was one of the best stock horses I ever saw when Joe Fallon bought him. But he isn't now. Remember this, Orrin, *a horse gets to be just like his master* . . . You won't see Fallon around here after today."

The cluster of men in front of the chutes passed similar remarks among themselves and then good-humoredly began to start other activities.

Blacky's face relaxed, and eagerness shone in his black eyes again as he said to Orrin, "They're getting up a race. You'll want to watch this—it will be good."

A wiry young man on a buckskin beckoned to Blacky. "Y'all want to ride my hoss?" he drawled. "I'll kick in the entry price and we'll split the winnings."

Blacky refused the offer, although Orrin thought that he did so reluctantly.

"Each fellow in the race puts up a dollar," Blacky explained, "and the winner takes the pot." He added apologetically, "A man my age shouldn't even think of racing."

In gay spirits the contestants lined up their horses, which seemed as keen for the race as were the men. Orrin decided that the young man on the buckskin would win. The start was swift. The cow ponies were of the famed quarter horse type, bred to run at top speed for short distances. They jumped to their best strides immediately, their powerfully muscled shoulders driving, driving.

As they charged toward the finish, all closely bunched, a red-faced fellow on a bay managed to push his mount ahead of the buckskin. He grinned boyishly as he collected the money, while the owner of the buckskin talked to his disappointed-looking horse and gave him an encouraging pat on his rump.

"This is more fun than milking cows," Blacky chuckled. "But I reckon we better think about getting back home."

"What about your business in Oklahoma City?" Orrin asked.

"Oh—oh, yes," Blacky replied, a little confused. He shifted slightly as if to leave, but clearly he had no notion of going as yet.

Orrin was delighted to stay in the arena. His eyes followed the riders enviously as they milled about, waiting for a new batch of calves to be run up to the chutes. The skill with which the men rode made the boy determine that some day he would ride equally as well.

A little farther along the fence three horses blinked drowsily in the sun while they waited for their masters. He stepped over to them to make friends with them, but they stood passive while he talked to them, and acted neither friendly nor hostile. They continued to swish their tails, but the sensitiveness that Orrin had become accustomed to in Golden Cloud and Queen was noticeably lacking in these horses.

"Want to borrow my horse?" a pleasant man in a tan leather jacket called. "She can take plenty of running."

"No, thanks, not today," Orrin replied, not wanting to explain that he was a poor rider. At the first opportunity he moved back toward Blacky.

Two men were talking to him, evidently trying to persuade him to do something that was not too unattractive.

"Oh, all right, you old cattle rustlers!" Blacky was saying as Orrin got there.

"Just wait around," Blacky told him, "these fellows have me hog-tied with their slick talk. Nothing will satisfy them but that I get into this calf roping."

"You going to hunt leather and back out?" One of the men challenged.

Blacky, already on his way to another part of the arena, pretended he could not hear.

"That's Blacky Martin," the same man said to Orrin. "The fellow that cracked down on Joe Fallon. I reckon maybe you know him."

Orrin noticed the respect in the man's voice as he mentioned Blacky's name.

"I work for him," Orrin replied.

"Sure 'nough?" the other said with a lift of his eyebrows. "I've seen old Blacky take top money at rodeos all the way from San Antone to Calgary . . . How's yourself—pretty handy with a loop?"

Orrin felt embarrassed again. He replied, "No, not so good."

The other gave him a knowing look. "Bulldogger?"

"I guess I'm nothing much of anything."

"Modest like Blacky, eh?" After a moment he rambled on, "Too bad Blacky never made out raising horses. For all he knows about them, he just can't keep his mind on business . . . Good thing he married Clara. She's one in a thousand, that woman. Shucks, she can even keep Blacky hobbled on practice days—that is, most of the time. One thing she can't do is get rid of Gabe. Blacky promised to look after Gabe until he's turned twenty-five. He ought to be near growed up by then." The flow of gossip ended when Blacky reappeared.

"So this is our business trip to Oklahoma City," Orrin thought, as Blacky took the other men across the arena with him. There was a reckless, devil-may-care bearing about Blacky that Orrin could not help but see. The rancher was in his element now, a different man from the one who rode the tractor or mended the fence.

Orrin watched the three men walk over to a sorrel that was tied to the front of an empty chute. Nothing that Blacky did escaped the boy's attentive eyes—the way he rocked the saddle, tightened the cinches, adjusted the stirrups and swung up on the horse.

Blacky was now guiding the sorrel in a narrow circle. Satisfied with this much of the procedure, he galloped halfway down the arena, whirling a lasso. Then he jogged back, carelessly holding the saddle horn with his right hand.

One by one the men who had tried their skill at calf roping earlier rode again until Blacky's turn came. The figures that had been leaning against the chutes digging designs in the dust with their high heels threw away their cigarette butts and straightened up as Blacky backed the sorrel into the far chute.

"Two bits that you can't beat twenty-five seconds," one of them called to Blacky.

"That ole sorrel is a top horse," Orrin heard another man remark. "I'll give him twenty-two."

Blacky had a piece of cord in his teeth, and the lasso ready in his right hand. He steadied the eager horse, and nodded to the men sitting on the next railing. One of them opened the gate and a calf streaked out.

As soon as the starter pulled the rope barrier, the sorrel plunged ahead.

"Ride that horse!" someone shouted as Blacky's mount tore after the calf.

"Look at that pony lay her ears back and run!" chuckled the spectator nearest Orrin.

The chase was brief, however. Before the calf had a

chance to start dodging, Blacky's loop swooshed over its head. The sorrel's hoofs plowed up the dust, and Blacky, with loose shirttail waving, raced down the rope and reached for the calf's foreleg.

"Yippee!" Orrin heard his own excited yell mingle with other cries of approval.

Amid the surprised grunts and bawling of the calf, Blacky snatched the cord from his teeth and whipped it around three of the calf's feet. An instant later he stepped clear and jerked his hands up above his head.

"Sixteen and two-tenths seconds," the man with a watch shouted. The word passed from mouth to mouth. There was a mark for the others to shoot at!

At least an hour passed before Blacky remembered that he had other obligations. In the meantime he had roped another calf while riding a different horse; although his time was slightly slower, he showed the same dexterity as before. Between rides he lounged with friends and offered useful tips to men with poorly trained mounts.

The light in Blacky's eyes was slowly dimming as he joined Orrin and headed for the pickup. He seemed to remember his shirttail, for he reached behind, caught at it and made a weak attempt to tuck it inside his trousers. After he walked a few steps, it fell out again, but Blacky seemed to feel he had done his duty and therefore paid no more attention to it.

"I shouldn't have kept you waiting so long," he muttered to Orrin. "Those fellows could sell dry ice to Eskimos. They plumb talked me into trying out their horses."

Orrin reflected that Blacky had been an easy subject for their arguments, but aloud he said with genuine enthusiasm, "You certainly did a swell job of roping. Won first prize, didn't you?"

Blacky shrugged his shoulders. "As old as I am, I ought to know enough to stay out of there." But the flare-up of excitement in his eyes contradicted his words.

After the pickup had lurched out of the parking space, Orrin was content to lean back in silence against the hard cushions. The visit to the Frontier Club had given him much to think about, and his thoughts kept turning over in his mind like colored objects in a child's toy. His unhappy life with Uncle Chauncey occasionally tumbled up on top, but he tried to submerge this recollection hastily. For the most part he reflected on the expert horsemanship and skillful roping he had seen, caught once more the cowed look on Joe Fallon's face when Blacky had reprimanded him. No matter how brusque Blacky was at times, he would not stand for the mistreatment of a horse. Orrin could not help feeling grateful that Golden Cloud was owned by him instead of by someone like Fallon.

Blacky, still keyed up, meanwhile conducted a one-sided conversation to which Orrin answered absently with grunts, until he heard the filly mentioned.

"Gabe and I will try her out tomorrow and see if she is as smart as Queen," Blacky chuckled. "It's time she struck up a speaking acquaintance with a halter shank."

Orrin's face beamed. "Don't worry about her. She'll learn fast enough." Then his smile faded as the picture of Gabe Martin came to mind. He had forgotten about Gabe in the excitement of the afternoon—forgotten that Gabe would be staying at Sunset Hill and Orrin would soon be moving along, forgotten that perhaps he would lose the little palomino.

6. A Promise Is Made

"**B**LACKY is going to give you your first lesson today,"
Orrin told Golden Cloud before he started to give
Queen her morning grooming.

Golden Cloud merely tilted her head and blinked
and continued to tag along with Orrin, reaching out
occasionally to nibble at the boy's hand. He noticed
Queen's ears prick up, as they always did, at a certain
footstep. Then he heard her quick whinny as she welcomed Blacky Martin into the stable.

"You can tell whose horse she is," Orrin remarked as
Queen showed delight in Blacky's attention. He added
with a wistfulness that Blacky did not catch, "But this
little filly is mine. She's my buddy."

"She *has* taken to you, at that," Blacky admitted ab-
sentmindedly, as he laid a rasp and a knife on the floor.

"I'm going to trim the little one's hoofs while we're waiting for Gabe."

"Where did Gabe go?" Orrin asked hopefully. There might be a lucky chance that Gabe would not return soon. In that event Orrin could help with Cloud's first lesson.

"Gabe's waltzed off somewhere to look at stock again," Blacky replied aloud. He lifted Golden Cloud's hoof and mused with head down, "Funny thing, Gabe hasn't bought a single mare. Maybe Clara is right. Maybe Gabe's talk about breeding horses in Texas is just plain hogwash."

"What did you say?" Orrin asked.

"Nothing," Blacky replied sharply. "I was thinking." He pointed to the soft portion in the middle of Golden Cloud's hoof. "See here? This is the frog, and it's mighty tender. Be sure to keep it clean and free from sharp stones, or one day you'll find yourself with a lame filly. Best to trim hoofs once a month. You'll get the hang of it before long.

"Now then," he went on after he had carefully trimmed the margins of the frogs, "let's see how the young lady is going to like being led. There's a colt halter hanging in the tack room. Bring that and a couple of lead shanks. We won't wait for Gabe."

Orrin ran to the tack room and whistled a tune under his breath while he reached for the gear. In a moment he was back, but Blacky was no longer in the stable. Orrin glanced about perplexed, walked through the box stall and looked outdoors. Over by the paddock gate Blacky was talking to Gabe, and near by, tied to the fence, stood a young chestnut filly.

Disappointed at seeing Gabe, Orrin slumped down on the doorstep to wait, laying the tack on the ground beside him. The two men continued to talk, and Orrin kept watching the filly until curiosity made him get up and walk over toward her.

Orrin passed near Blacky and Gabe, but neither noticed him. Gabe's face was flushed, his hat pushed back on his curly hair, a thumb hooked in his belt. Blacky's expression was inscrutable. His eyes were narrowed and his voice brittle as he answered Gabe. Orrin moved past them and began to make friends with the filly.

The foal was attractive, like all young animals, and he eagerly stroked her head and felt the smoothness of her coat as he sought to win her confidence. "You're a pretty little thing," he crooned, unconsciously using Blacky's expression. "Look at this. You have a tiny white patch on your flank." He studied the mark closely and then grinned as the foal nuzzled his hand. With all her appeal, he could not help comparing her with Golden Cloud. There had always been an exciting quality about Cloud's beauty that this filly could not begin to match. But then, he thought, there would never be another filly who could.

The voices of the men were becoming louder now, and Orrin heard them clearly. Gabe was talking petulantly. "You don't want me to make out at breeding horses, just because *you* couldn't. You never did aim to help me when I needed it."

"You've had a home here for the past seven years," Blacky retorted.

"Yeah," Gabe said bitterly, "and in three more years you won't have to be bothered with me any more."

"I promised Dad I'd see you through ten years," Blacky snapped, "and I'll keep my word. With three years to go, I reckon it's time you began to get started on your own."

"You've got a boy to help you now and don't need me?"

"I never did need you." Blacky's voice showed that his temper was running short.

Gabe grumbled something, and his voice took on a crafty, wheedling tone. "Give me Queen and you can forget about me."

"Queen!" Blacky exploded.

"Well, the filly then."

"Golden Cloud?"

"Why not? Queen will drop another foal next year. Remember what you promised your father." There was a cunning persuasiveness in Gabe's voice. "You told him you'd help me learn kindness to horses. I've changed, Blacky. I'll gentle her. I see things different now. All I need is a chance. Give me the filly, Blacky, and you'll be helping to keep your word to your father."

Orrin's fingers stroked the chestnut's mane unfeelingly. Blacky was hesitating over Gabe's request, and it frightened Orrin. He had not known about Blacky's promises to his father. Cloud might as well be given to Joe Fallon as to Gabe.

"I want to help you," Blacky said stubbornly. "I gave Dad my word. But Golden Cloud is right valuable."

"More valuable than your promise to a dying man?"

"Let me talk to Clara first. She was saying something—"

"You're a man, and the little palomino belongs to you, not to Clara. Make up your own mind, Blacky."

Blacky's hesitation seemed endless to Orrin.

At last the rancher said, "You can have her—on condition."

"What is it?" Gabe cried.

"Bring me that little chestnut filly in three years. If she's sound and gentle and properly broken, I'll give you Golden Cloud."

"Three years!" Gabe burst out. "You're fooling."

"That's my offer," Blacky said flatly, "and you know I'll stand by it."

Gabe started to protest, but the expression on Blacky's face showed that he would not budge. Besides, Gabe must have known he had made an excellent deal as it was, for he began to grin as he turned toward the chestnut filly.

For the first time Gabe seemed to notice Orrin. He growled at the boy, "You here sticking your big nose in other people's business again?"

Orrin realized Gabe was partly justified in what he said, so he merely replied quietly, "I came over to take a look at your horse."

"Gabe, come along," Blacky called as he headed for Queen's stall. While Gabe went with Blacky, Orrin ran through the tack room and inside the stable, where he could watch over the top of the door. He was just beginning to realize the full meaning of Blacky's promise to Gabe.

Golden Cloud bobbed her head uncertainly while Blacky buckled on the halter, but she made no strenuous resistance. Blacky passed one of the halter shanks to Gabe. "Snap this on Queen's bridle and walk her slow into the paddock. I'll lead the filly along behind. Take it easy now, and don't let her get excited."

Taking up the slack of the halter shank with a loop in his left hand, Gabe grasped the line close to the bridle, kicked open the outside door, and led Queen into the paddock. As she thumped out of the stall, the light footfalls of Golden Cloud sounded behind her.

"Walk her around in a circle," Blacky directed.

Orrin was now watching at the outside door. His breathing had quickened, partly from excitement and partly because Gabe was doing what he himself had hoped to do.

As Gabe turned left, Golden Cloud suddenly showed her objecting to being led. Up she reared on her slender legs, fighting the disagreeable leather and metal trap that robbed her of her freedom. He held Queen back while Blacky handled the line, keeping the filly's head straight ahead. Meanwhile, he talked to her and in a minute Golden Cloud quieted down, and they continued traveling in a slow circle. But Golden Cloud was not ready to submit so easily. From both Queen and her Arabian sire she had inherited intelligence, but she had also inherited a love of independence. It annoyed her to trail at the end of a rope behind her mother; she wanted to be at Queen's side. If this man could not understand, she would have to break away from him. She reared again, fighting harder than ever.

"You're kicking up those hoofs more than I thought you would," Blacky grunted, coolly managing the line to avoid injury to the filly. "Maybe you're not so smart as we figured."

"Let me take her," Gabe offered. "She'll lead for me."

"You're always so cocksure of yourself," Blacky muttered, but he exchanged lines.

Orrin turned his head away for a moment as he saw the gloating way in which Gabe looked at Cloud.

Once more the slow procession started, but this time it stopped for a different reason. Golden Cloud began favoring her right foreleg, and Blacky's sharp eye saw the motion. "Hold up," he called to Gabe. "Something is wrong with her foot.

"It isn't trimmed too close," he said as he examined the hoof. "No sign of a pebble there. It can't be that she's tricking me—young as she is. I wonder what's the trouble." They went a little farther, but the same slight limp developed.

Orrin could not stand still any longer. "Let me try her," he yelled. "She's used to me."

Gabe glared, and Blacky looked up at him with a frown. "If her leg is really bad," the rancher said, "we shouldn't aggravate it; and if she's faking, there's no telling what she would do with you on the line."

"I'll be careful," Orrin pleaded.

Blacky was annoyed, but he gave in. "Let him take her, Gabe."

Gabe gave him a hard look as he released the halter shank, but Orrin's gaze was on Cloud and he missed Gabe's displeasure.

The filly's ears twitched as Orrin approached her and her eyes softened. He reached for her head and patted the patches of gold that shone between the strips of leather.

"All right," Blacky conceded, "keep your eye on her." He gave a slight pull on Queen's halter.

With Orrin's hand on the rope, Golden Cloud behaved like a different animal. She still preferred to be at Queen's flank, but if Orrin wanted her to stay behind, that was where she would stay. Her limp was entirely gone and, although she showed signs of restiveness under the close control, there was no more rearing.

"I can't believe it," Blacky said. "Let me take her again."

At once the limp reappeared. "It's the strangest thing I ever saw," the amazed Blacky admitted. He was not fully convinced until they had traded horses again and Golden Cloud once more lost her limp.

"Dumb luck," Gabe muttered. "I'll go where I am needed." He stalked across the paddock and untied the chestnut filly. The next time Orrin looked in that direction both Gabe and his filly were gone.

After a few more rounds, Blacky was satisfied. "We

won't try leading her in front of Queen today," he said. "She's had enough. Take it slow, but keep at it—that's the way to train horses."

Orrin removed Golden Cloud's halter and watched her scamper away to enjoy the freedom of the entire paddock. He remembered her fake limp and he shook his head, enormously pleased to think the filly would trust him when she wouldn't even behave for the veteran horseman, Blacky Martin.

Blacky watched Golden Cloud gallop about with the sunlight flashing on her sleek form. He turned to Orrin and said brusquely, "I've promised her to Gabe, so don't let yourself get too attached to her." As Blacky left, he carefully tucked his loose shirttail inside his trousers. This he never did except in deference to Clara. Perhaps he was going to talk to her now about his promise to Gabe, Orrin mused.

After Blacky had gone and Orrin had turned Queen into an adjoining pasture, the boy stood for a long time leaning on the fence and staring at Cloud. That dark, brooding light was back in his eyes. There were things about ranch life that could give one the same helpless feeling and hurt just as deeply as anything in the city. Right now neither way of life seemed tolerable to Orrin. With one abrupt motion he drew away from the fence.

He was cleaning out the stable and trying to persuade himself that in three years time he would completely forget about Golden Cloud and the Martins, when he heard the clomp of Ripple's shoes echoing inside the barn. The moody feeling within him increased.

"Hey, there, hired help, where are you?" Gabe called.

Orrin pushed his way through the slatted door to

the main barn. The muscles of his mouth and jaws were taut, but he spoke civilly, "You want me?"

Gabe's face was turned away for a moment as he dismounted from Ripple. Orrin waited, afraid he would lose his temper if Gabe asked him to rub down his horse. However, he was greeted by a chuckle from Gabe. "You're such a top hand with horses, I stopped by to see if you all would like to take a little ride on Ripple. She's still fresh."

"No thanks," Orrin replied shortly, for he could tell that Gabe was furious about what had happened during Cloud's lesson.

"I never did see you on a horse," Gabe continued. "You'd like to jump her over the gate, wouldn't you? I'll take down the top bar and make it right easy."

Orrin turned away wearily with only a shake of his head.

"Come on," Gabe teased. "Just one little jump to show me you're a great big cowboy."

A hot rush of blood surged through Orrin's body. He stopped suddenly, all reason driven away by Gabe's words, and strode back to Ripple. He shortened the stirrups with hands that trembled in anger. He knew that much about jumping. Then he walked around to the paddock and threw open the gate to make the jump from the inside, where there was room for a start.

At that moment the hot-headed impulse to answer Gabe's dare left him. He thought more clearly of the broken bones that might result. In addition to the thought of physical pain was the thought that he did not have the money to carry him through such an emergency. While he deliberated, he caught another glimpse of Gabe's face. That was enough to push aside all thoughts of danger to himself.

Orrin steadied Ripple now as best he could and concentrated on the ordeal ahead of him. His close observation of others had told him to throw his weight with the jump and to give the horse free rein over the gate. Experimentally he crouched over Ripple's neck, getting the feel of the stirrups and gripping hard with his knees against the warm body.

Gabe's wilful riding had not improved Ripple's disposition. She was usually even-tempered and calm, but now she danced nervously and tossed her head as Orrin pulled her around and faced the bars. There was no use in delaying, he reasoned, when the sorrel's fidgeting had quited down. From this point on, a great deal depended on luck. He gripped the reins and squeezed against the sorrel's ribs with his legs.

Ripple understood what was expected of her and started forward, jerking her rider off balance by the suddenness of her start. Orrin was quick to catch himself, but the distance to the gate was closing swiftly. He thought now that he had been foolish to let Gabe taunt him into trying the jump. But the gate was directly in their path, and worrying about it would do no good, so he gave Ripple her head, and held his breath.

Handicapped by her rider's uncertainty, Ripple jumped awkwardly, clearing the gate but stumbling as she landed. Orrin had leaned forward as the mare sprang, and for a thrilling moment believed he would make it. But with the break in the horse's rhythm as she stumbled, he felt his weight heave irresistibly forward, and he knew in a vague way that he was pitching to the ground.

Instinctively he threw his hands out and relaxed as he had been taught to do when tackled in football scrimmage. A hard hand seemed to whack him, throwing thick, smothering dust into his mouth as he started to roll in the ground.

As the haze in Orrin's head began to clear, the details of the jump came back to him one by one. Then he realized that he was on his hands and knees, shaking his head dazedly and wondering what the pain in his shoulder meant. At the same instant he heard a voice above him. Gabe was standing over him, his expression showing relief, but his voice unpleasant. "Feel like you'd want to go back to *De*-troit about now?"

Orrin looked up, but ignored the question and moved his shoulder gingerly. He worked his arm slightly and then drew an easier breath. The shoulder was painfully sore, but he had suffered no serious injury.

Meanwhile, Gabe, seeing that Orrin was able to get back to work, mounted Ripple and leisurely rode away.

Although the stiffness wore out of Orrin's shoulder as the afternoon moved along, his thoughts and actions were listless. He was helping Mrs. Martin wash the supper dishes that evening when Gabe appeared, in none too good a mood.

"Your hired man is mighty handy around the kitchen," Gabe remarked significantly.

"He's a hard worker and earns his wages," Mrs. Martin replied quietly.

Gabe's rejoinder was addressed to Blacky rather than to Mrs. Martin. "He earns his keep and I don't—is that the general idea?"

"Keep your shirt on," Blacky urged. "Orrin has been right useful around here."

"Leave this buckaroo around the horses much longer and there won't be any left to work with," Gabe grunted. "He can't even ride."

"He wasn't hired because he could ride," Blacky replied gruffly.

Orrin recognized the fairness in Blacky's reply, but he

could not forget that Blacky had promised to give Golden Cloud to his cousin.

Gabe muttered something and strode into the living room. Troubled lines appeared faintly in Mrs. Martin's usually smooth forehead.

"You two don't get along very well," was all she said to Orrin.

Blacky excused himself and went outside while Orrin and Mrs. Martin finished the dishes. A few minutes later Gabe walked through the kitchen and down the back steps on his way to visit a friend.

"You haven't felt content since Gabe came, have you?" Mrs. Martin asked Orrin as she folded her towel carefully over the rack.

"Oh, he doesn't bother me much!" Orrin replied dully. "I won't be here much longer anyway, so why should I worry?"

Mrs. Martin looked at him quickly. "We haven't asked you to leave."

Orrin's expression was dogged. "I might as well go get myself another job. Gabe will pitch in here as soon as I'm not around."

"Nobody knows whether Gabe will stay on and work. We'll have to be patient and put up with him and his ways for—for Blacky's sake." She looked thoughtfully at Orrin for a moment. "You've gotten mighty fond of that little filly, haven't you?"

Orrin grunted, "Uh-huh," and stared into the sink.

"I know about Golden Cloud," Mrs. Martin said quietly. "Blacky did it only because of a promise to his father—and Gabe will have to prove himself before he gets Cloud. Honestly, I don't think he will make good. Orrin, I want you to stay on here as a regular hand. Gabe's visits never last long, and you're more help than you think. I'm depending on you to stay, Orrin."

In his indecision he felt the power of Mrs. Martin's affection for him. He made no reply, and Mrs. Martin seemed to expect none. Yet both knew that he had been convinced against his better judgment to remain.

7. A Fair Fight

Early the next morning Orrin talked to Golden Cloud as Queen munched her grain. "I'm not quitting," he said soberly to the horse. "Mrs. Martin says it's best for me to stay."

He was interrupted in his reverie by the quick movement of Golden Cloud, who suddenly decided to dash the tiny distance to the far corner of the stall. She stopped as suddenly as she had started and looked back at Orrin with a comical tilt to her head.

He pretended to scold her. "You're getting too big for such nonsense, Cloud. Look at the size of you!"

Her round, young eyes were so appealing that he strode over and caught her head playfully between his hands. Golden Cloud tugged back and Orrin's finger brushed the sensitive inside of her ear. She gave her head a vigorous shake that amused him. "That's the first time you ever said *no* to me. Maybe you think you are one of these educated horses, do you?"

Out of curiosity, Orrin tickled Golden Cloud's ear again and again she shook her head. "Say, I could teach you to do that for a trick," he said aloud, half seriously.

A deep-throated laugh suddenly resounded through the top half of the stable door. Gabe stood there with a sardonic grin on his face. "Taking right hold of things, eh?" he drawled. "I reckon you're aiming to be just like Sonny Le May with his trick horse. They say there's plenty money in that business."

From behind Gabe, Blacky's voice came like the slap of a quirt, as if he and his cousin had been quarreling. "Maybe he'll do just that, Gabe. You can teach a growing filly a heap more than some people think."

"When I get to own that palomino, I want a horse, not a trained poodle," Gabe replied sulkily.

"Don't worry," Blacky snapped, "she'll be trained right."

The wrangling between Blacky and Gabe continued as they moved along, their voices growing gradually fainter in the passageway.

When Orrin led Queen out to pasture, he saw the chestnut filly already in the field. At least Gabe was finding time to take care of her. As she frisked from one grazing spot to another, Orrin watched her. He could not help frowning when he thought of the end of the three-year period, and he wondered what she would be like in that time.

From day to day he continued to go about his duties as he always had, hard working and observant, while Gabe quarreled often with Blacky and spoke vaguely about returning to Texas. Orrin tried not to think about Gabe's hold on Golden Cloud, but it clung in the back of his mind like a storm cloud that drifts along the horizon, distant but dark.

Gabe's treatment of Ripple and the other horses had been above criticism until one morning when he and Blacky quarreled with unusual bitterness. A hour later Orrin saw Gabe storm out of the barn with a saddle, but he did not stop to watch what Gabe was going to do.

For the rest of the morning Orrin worked at the cow barn, whitewashing the walls. Just before noon he ran down to the barn for a spare length of garden hose, and he saw Ripple tied outside the big door. Orrin caught a quick glimpse of lather and perspiration, but the thing that startled him was a series of red welts on her sides where spurs had raked her. When he looked up, he saw Gabe, catching him with an expression in which furtiveness and defiance were merged.

"What are you staring at?" Gabe blustered. "She got scratched going through the brush."

Orrin's glance turned toward Gabe's boots. He thought he saw dark stains on the rowels of his spurs, but Gabe shuffled his feet and moved about when he saw Orrin's steady gaze.

"Well, don't try to make something of it," Gabe growled. "And don't think that Blacky wants you to run to him with stories either."

Ripple's hard breathing sounded for an interval. Orrin guessed that what Gabe had said about Blacky was right, but somebody should try to correct Gabe.

"It's pretty rough on a horse to be ridden so hard. Why don't you take it easier, Gabe? Horses have the same feelings as people."

Gabe's eyes flared, but he quickly assumed a more humble attitude. "She isn't as bad off as she looks. I used to be hard on horses—sometimes. No more. When I finish rubbing her down, she'll be fresh as a bluebonnet. Those scratches could stand a touch of iodine. Don't worry. I'll take care of her."

Orrin found the hose he had come for and returned to the cow barn. Gabe was going to rub down his own horse for a change. That was something! But here was another thought! The more gentle Gabe became with horses, the surer he was to get Cloud. Maybe Orrin was actually helping Gabe to win the palomino!

That idea made Orrin frown, but no matter what happened, he couldn't stand by and let a fellow be cruel to a horse.

Judging by Gabe's surliness at lunch time, he was very much annoyed at Orrin. Blacky suggested that Gabe clean out the gasoline line on the tractor some time during the afternoon. Gabe's immediate retort was, "I'll get to it if I have time."

Blacky answered calmly and evenly, "I thought you might be looking for something to do."

"You're always thinking up something for me to do. You sure don't like to see me have any fun."

Blacky's face tightened, but Clara interrupted with a smile, "We'd all like to have more fun, Gabe. I haven't been to a party myself since the Dawson wedding a year ago. Last time I was in Oklahoma City there was a ruffly dress in Brown's I admired. I'd have bought it too, if there weren't so many repairs to make at the dairy."

Gabe grunted something, and Orrin found himself staring at Mrs. Martin. He had never thought of her as caring for parties or fancy dresses. The rest of the meal passed without further outbreaks, but the conversation was noticeably strained.

In the early afternoon Blacky approached Orrin. "Son," he said bluntly, "how would you like to take a run to the Frontier Club? Sonny Le May will be there working out his trick horse. We'll be back by milking time."

Orrin agreed quickly. A change would be good today.

"I've been teaching Cloud to kneel," he said as the pickup rattled off. "I'm anxious to see what Le May's horse can do."

Blacky gave him a disapproving look. "I wouldn't try to make Cloud into a trick horse. We'll teach her to jump when she's old enough."

He pushed the pickup hard, disregarding the jolts, and said nothing more until they were passing a farm where the smell of hay blew across the road, and stands of wheat were turning golden ripe in the sunshine.

"A good day for haying," Blacky remarked, glancing at the nearest field. A hay baler was methodically kicking off bales of greenish hay and leaving them scattered about like huge, misshapen dice. "We'll make the most of our spree today, because tomorrow we'll be busy with our haying."

At the Frontier Club, Blacky parked his pickup and jumped out quickly. "There'll be a young fellow looking for me," he explained to Orrin, "but you come right inside and make yourself at home."

As they walked along the wire fence toward the chutes, Orrin watched a roper bearing down on a calf. Horse and rider worked nicely together as the loop settled over the calf's head. The cloud of dust kicked up by the horse's hoofs blew into his eyes, but he refused to turn his head away, as he did not want to miss any of the details.

No sooner had Blacky and Orrin passed through the gate into the arena, than a man on horseback, dressed in ordinary dress shirt, levis and sand-colored felt hat, touched his knees to his horse and cantered over. "Where you been keeping yourself," he grinned at Blacky as he pulled up his horse. "Haven't seen you for a while."

Blacky seemed a little embarrassed to be reminded in front of Orrin that in the past he had frequented the club so often, but he was all business as he asked, "You been working with this little bay right along, Corb?"

"Sure have. I've been waiting for you to try her out." Corb gave his horse a pat. "She's still green," he said proudly, "but she's sure going to be a slick cow pony when we get through training her." He dismounted and stood aside so Blacky could ride her.

"How do you like her?" Corb asked Orrin as Blacky jogged off.

"Swell," Orrin replied. He knew better than to attempt to go into details in such expert company.

Blacky was soon back, talking to his friend about feed and training and saddles.

"Try her out on a calf," the young man kept urging him.

Blacky agreed reluctantly. "I shouldn't do this," he remarked to Orrin. "A man gets rusty when he doesn't keep at this game." But he went to work adjusting the cinches and shortening the stirrups. "I'll work with her a little while first," he said, as he glanced doubtfully at the bay.

While Blacky and Corb schooled the bay, Orrin walked toward an empty chute where he would be out of the way. He was standing there alone when a gray sedan pulling a horse trailer stopped by the gate. A light-complexioned young man with a round, smooth face got out, walked to the back of the trailer, and presently led a horse into the arena.

Orrin looked at the animal, a flea-bitten gray stallion, which the man was leading by a rope. He saw that the horse was not saddled. This must be Sonny Le May and his trick horse, Orrin guessed. It gave him a thrill to see this horse, although it was coarse-boned and not distinguished-looking in any way except for a pair of very intelligent eyes.

A group of youngsters who had been chasing one another behind the chutes called to Le May by name and immediately climbed over the chutes. Sonny Le May waved to them and grinned, obviously pleased by their admiring glances.

"Make him lie down," a boy shouted.

There was no calf roping going on at that moment, so Le May obliged. A signal from his master's hands, and the gray sat down, bent his forelegs, and rolled over. Another boy, familiar with the horse's repertoire, called out, "Now go to sleep with him."

Le May curled up against the horse's belly, pulled his hat over his eyes, and began to snore. The gray jerked back his heavy foreleg and bumped Le May. In pretended annoyance, the man roused himself and pushed back the leg. He settled himself for another nap, only to be disturbed a second time in the same way. A chuckle passed around the growing circle of men and boys who crowded around to watch.

Bright-eyed, Orrin slipped through to the front row of the group, while Le May put his horse through one trick after another.

"How old are you, Skipper?" Le May asked the stallion.

The horse solemnly stamped his right front hoof five times. Orrin thought he detected a slight motion of Le May's head at each count, but was not sure. Between tricks, he talked to some of the men, calling each one of them by name. From the conversation Orrin learned that Skipper performed at many of the smaller rodeos, and that he was going to be featured at the coming rodeo of the Frontier Club.

It was the first time Orrin had ever seen a trick horse perform, and he followed every movement of Le May and Skipper intently. The response of the horse to commands was uncanny. Each time that Le May was particularly pleased with a trick, he would reach into his trouser pocket for a morsel of food that the horse would seize avidly from his outstretched palm.

Finally, Le May had Skipper conclude his tricks with several poses. Some of the men returned to calf roping, but Orrin stayed close to Le May and watched his chance to get in a question.

"Is it hard to teach a horse tricks?"

"It takes patience mostly," Le May drawled, "and a liking for horses. Some horses take to it easier than others. This fellow has always been quick to catch on. Show him a piece of bread, and he'd try to stand on his head to get it."

"They like to be rewarded?"

"Sure."

"How do they know what you want them to do?"

"Well, when you first start teaching them, always use some kind of signal. Skipper has gotten so he can usually tell what to do by the tone of my voice."

Other boys, anxious to talk with the trick-horse trainer, took over the conversation. But Orrin was satisfied just to listen and to admire. A glamour had enveloped Le May's person, seeming to hold him at an uncertain, wavering distance, although he actually stood within arm's reach. A pale glow illumined his smooth face, which constantly widened and narrowed according to the depth of his smile. Of all the colorful horsemen whom Orrin had met so far, Sonny Le May certainly ranked highest.

Eventually Le May decided to move along; he had an appointment for four o'clock. His parting remark was addressed to Orrin, who evidently impressed him as the most interested of his spectators.

"Let me take a look at your horse after you've trained him," Le May drawled. His face broadened pleasantly under his shining aura.

"I will," Orrin promised. "I sure will if you're around."

He slowly walked away by himself, anxious to be alone with a dream that had dazzled him for the moment.

"Why not?" he asked himself. "Cloud is smarter than Skipper and ten times as pretty. Blacky himself says that a young horse can be taught a lot."

A stirring picture expanded in Orrin's mind. He and Golden Cloud were facing a huge crowd that clamored for their act to begin. It was more wonderful than anything he had ever imagined before. Loud voices near by suddenly aroused him from his dreaming. He looked up abruptly. Directly in front of him he saw the sunburned face and broad shoulders of Gabe Martin.

Gabe greeted him with pretended friendliness, and hooked his arm through Orrin's, and led the boy toward a group of the younger men, evidently his cronies.

"This is our hired help," Gabe grinned. "If you ask him real pretty, maybe he'll give you an exhibition of jumping."

The faces that Orrin saw in front of him showed mild amusement. One of them asked with a lazy smile, "Want to borrow my horse, Bub?"

Orrin tried to grin. There was no use being a bad sport about it.

"I can jump better without a horse," he laughed.

"That's the spirit," a thickset man in a green shirt said good-naturedly, "don't let old Gabe play any of his tricks on you."

Taking advantage of the laugh that followed, Orrin told Gabe that he would see him later. He gave a pull to release his arm, but Gabe would not let go. It was clear that Gabe's resentment toward Orrin had never stopped increasing. Orrin's lips closed in a tight, obstinate line.

"Remember what I was telling you about bulldogging

steers in Texas?" Gabe asked the young men. "I'll show you what I meant."

Before Orrin understood the other's intentions, Gabe slipped his arm farther through Orrin's, and making use of the increased leverage, gave a quick twist. In order to avoid a wrenched shoulder, Orrin had to give with the thrust. As he plunged into the thick dust, Gabe chuckled, "It's as easy as that when you know how."

Orrin rose slowly, fighting for control of himself. So far he had done his best to get along amicably with Gabe. He had accepted slights quietly, and he had overlooked taunts. Now Gabe was ridiculing him in public. Through a reddish haze Orrin studied Gabe's powerful build; he remembered feats of strength the other had performed to show his superiority.

None of Gabe's friends laughed at the way he had taken advantage of Orrin. One of them even drawled, "Well, you've sure shown us how to bulldog a steer. Suppose you set the poor critter loose now."

They turned in surprise as Orrin's voice broke through the laughter. "I didn't quite see how you did that, Gabe. Show me again."

The man in the green shirt stepped forward with a soft-spoken rebuke. "He's just a kid, Gabe. Better let him alone before you hurt him."

Gabe pushed the man aside roughly, faced Orrin, and cried with a wilful twist to his mouth, "You asked for it." As he did so, he lunged harder than was necessary for the boy's arm.

The moment Gabe's arm darted out, Orrin's anger cooled. He seized Gabe's wrist and upper arm, dragging down hard. As Gabe partly turned and stumbled a surprised half-step forward, Orrin dove for the outthrust leg and wrapped his left arm around it. Deftly he swung behind his opponent, where he grabbed both insteps and drove Gabe face downward into the dirt.

Orrin's first reactions had been instinctive; the movements of a trained wrestler taking advantage of a mistake. But Gabe, angered by the counterattack, used his strength savagely in an effort to break away. Orrin hastily decided on wrestling strategy. No use trying to pin his opponent while he was still dangerously fresh. Instead, he would try to stay on top and ride him until he was worn out.

With Gabe heaving as desperately as an unbroken horse, Orrin was forced to use every device of strength and skill to hook his legs around Gabe's, at the same time holding the other's wrists in a double bar lock. Once this grip was secured, he held on, attempting to force Gabe to exhaust his strength.

Gabe lay silent for a moment, gathering his energy for a violent attempt to unseat his rider. Orrin was ready when the outburst came. Although he rocked and tossed from the force of the assault, he pushed upward with his heels, continuing the punishment until Gabe subsided.

Gabe panted hard, while rivulets of perspiration ran down the side of his face and trickled off to form slowly widening blotches of mud. "Let me up and fight fair," he gasped into the earth.

"It was your idea," Orrin replied grimly. "There's nothing unfair about this hold."

"You're right, boy," a voice above Orrin reassured him. "He started it." Orrin glanced appreciatively at the speaker and realized for the first time that a circle of men and boys surrounded him. Others spoke in his defense, cheering him up immensely.

He heard somebody in the distance yell, "There goes Blacky! Watch him ride that pony!" Then in rage and humiliation Gabe pitched upward, and Orrin paid no attention to anyone else.

From side to side Gabe drove with his remaining strength, but Orrin always pushed his head in the opposite direction. When the storm finally ebbed, Gabe lay nearly helpless. Whether he was gasping or sobbing, Orrin could not be sure, but his fighting spirit was spent. Gabe raised his voice in exasperation, the final tones rising almost to a shriek, "Get off me, hear?"

"Make him say uncle," a bystander suggested.

"Looks like the steer bulldogged *him* this time," called another.

Gabe's voice was weary and without expression now. "Get off—get off—get—"

Orrin unhooked his legs and stepped clear, still wary of a trick on his opponent's part. Slowly Gabe rose, glancing sullenly about, and without a word limped off. Orrin watched him go, smeared with dirt and dust. The boy drew in a deep breath and half shook his head. Now what would this affair lead to at Sunset Hill Ranch?

Before he could visualize the possible outcome of the quarrel, he felt a hand pulling at his arm, and heard a voice in his ear crying, "You're here with Blacky Martin, aren't you?"

"Yes," Orrin said absently. "Why?"

"He's hurt!" the other said impatiently, "maybe bad—a horse just threw him."

The bad news increased the weak feeling in Orrin's tired body. "Where is he?"

"Yonder by chute No. 1."

Following the outstretched hand with his glance, Orrin saw two men kneeling over to examine a man's figure, small and limp, lying on the ground.

8. Facing an Emergency

BLACKY regained consciousness before the doctor arrived. But his dark, weather-scarred face had a grayish tinge and his eyes were glassy.

At last a black business coupé stopped outside the arena gate, and a man with a doctor's bag walked straight toward Blacky with brisk, businesslike stride. Orrin stood rigid and kept thinking of Clara Martin as the doctor's skilled fingers slid over Blacky's body. The possible results of their trip to the Frontier Club clouded Orrin's thoughts, indefinable, troublesome.

Behind the group of men near Blacky, several calves bawled mournfully as they milled about in their pen. Some of the younger boys had lost interest in the accident and were climbing over the chutes in a noisy game of tag. But the men talked in whispers as the doctor completed his examination.

The doctor finally stood up. "Phone the hospital for an ambulance," he said crisply to the fringe of men.

"Where's the nearest phone?" Orrin cried. He turned and started for the gate as the directions were shouted to him.

As he ran for the pickup, his thoughts came swifter, striking cruelly from all directions like a volley of flint-tipped arrows. He thought ahead to the moment when he must face Mrs. Martin and break to her the bad news about her husband. The image of Gabe's face, surly with hurt pride, momentarily pushed all other thoughts aside. Orrin could not find a single fragment of comfort anywhere.

As for the details of the ride itself, the boy could hardly remember any of them afterwards. They were all blurred in his haste to reach the nearest farmhouse, to put through the call and return to Blacky. Actually he had been gone only ten or fifteen minutes when he was again back at the arena.

The doctor had snapped his bag shut and was standing near Blacky, and watching the men return to their roping practice.

"The ambulance will be right here," Orrin said. He glanced at Blacky and then at the doctor with a question in his deep-set black eyes.

"Fractured collar bone and fracture of the right leg, definitely," the doctor stated briefly.

Orrin cleared his throat and tried not to act scared. "He'll come around all right?"

"Barring internal injuries," the doctor said softly so that Blacky could not hear. "X rays will tell the story."

"You mean—maybe—" the words trailed away, and he waited silently.

At last the thin scream of an ambulance siren sounded down the road. Blacky's eyelids quivered and opened when the attendants lifted him to the stretcher and carried him to the ambulance, but he made no attempt to talk. Orrin spoke to him, trying to sound cheerful, "Don't worry. I'll see that everything is taken care of at the ranch."

He left immediately for Sunset Hill, driving fast, but he could not help feeling worried about having to talk to Mrs. Martin. The time seemed unbelievably short before he found himself walking into the cow barn.

"It's been right lonesome around here all evening," Clara Martin said, smiling up at Orrin from a milking stool. "This is the first time in weeks you've been late for milking."

"Something happened—" Orrin began.

"I had a sort of feeling," Mrs. Martin began in a voice so quiet that Orrin could scarcely hear her. "Blacky makes believe he goes off on business, but it's the Frontier Club. One look at his shirttail and I can tell when he's been riding and roping." Her head bent lower, and her left hand shot streams of milk splashing harder into the milk bucket before she spoke again. "What was it, Orrin? Was he thrown from a horse?"

Orrin nodded. "Collar bone and right leg . . . They'll take X rays at the hospital."

Her slight body trembled a bit as she straightened on the stool, but her voice was firm. "I'll drive right over to the hospital, Orrin. You finish the milking." As she rose, she added with no trace of bitterness, "I'll drop a line to Andy Comfort in Chickasha after supper and tell him I'm not interested in his Jersey bull—doctors and hospitals use up a smart of money."

"Everything will turn out all right," Orrin assured her, for he did not know what else to say.

"Of course. Blacky's tough; this isn't the first time he was ever thrown. Don't you worry for a minute."

After she left, Orrin stared along the double row of stanchions where the cows unhurriedly nosed out the best hay. "It's a tough break for her," he muttered, as he thought of how Mrs. Martin had tried to belittle her own fears so that he would not be worried.

Orrin finished milking, turned the cows out to pasture, strained the milk and stored it in the cooler. His fingers and wrists were tired from the steady milking, but he was no longer frowning when Mrs. Martin returned.

"How is he?" he called as he ran to meet the pickup.

"He was resting nicely," Clara replied gently. "They still won't say much about his condition." She said nothing more for a few minutes. Then she smiled. "Blacky was feeling right ashamed of himself for being thrown. I reckon that's a hopeful sign."

Orrin and Clara Martin ate together in the kitchen that night. It reminded the boy of his first breakfast at the ranch. He had liked Mrs. Martin a lot even then, but he knew her much better now.

"About the haying," Mrs. Martin said briskly. "I'll ask Ike Johnson to lend me one of his men tomorrow and he can get you started. The grass is prime and the weather is just right . . . Of course, Gabe can help too—if he's around."

The next morning before daylight Orrin could hear Mrs. Martin's footsteps on the stairs. He was out of bed in an instant, pulling on his shirt and trousers, ashamed to think that she had gotten up before he did.

Clara's face appeared drawn in the gloom of early morning. It was apparent that she had slept poorly. "Gabe didn't come in at all last night," she said. "I hope nothing has happened to him."

It would have cheered Orrin to think that Gabe had

left for good, although he understood now that Gabe would be welcome at the ranch for at least another three years. He said thoughtfully, "He's probably spending the night with some friends."

"Likely so." A smile relieved the tension in Mrs. Martin's expression. "Maybe he heard about Blacky and wanted to stay near the hospital. It would make Blacky feel heaps better. After all, Gabe is his nearest relative."

Orrin and Mrs. Martin worked together steadily around the dairy until the cow barn was cleaned and the other chores finished. When she went back to the house to prepare breakfast, he dropped down to the stable. He glanced down the driveway, half expecting to see Gabe Martin arriving for breakfast, but nobody was in sight.

It was wonderful, the lifting sense of freedom that came to him when Gabe was not around. Even the morning wind, blowing warm and relentless from the south, felt invigorating. Orrin whistled as he walked into the barn, and Queen's shrill whinny answered him.

"Surprised to see me, aren't you?" he asked Queen as he reached for her grain pail. "I'm early."

The palomino's beautiful head followed Orrin's movements as he walked about the stall, and Golden Cloud, looking pert and frisky, pushed over with less dignity for her share of attention.

"I'll be back after breakfast," Orrin called to Golden Cloud after a farewell slap, "but don't expect to get as much attention as usual. We might have to skip a few lessons, too, but we'll go on with your training later."

Breakfast was ready when Orrin reached the kitchen. At sight of him, Mrs. Martin closed a ledger-type book with an abrupt motion, stepped to the stove and uncovered a pan that sizzled over a low flame. In it was country ham, skilfully spiced and rubbed with brown sugar. The aroma flooded the kitchen and made Orrin conscious of the hollowness of his stomach. He had been too busy to realize how hungry he was.

"Have you finished your breakfast already?" Orrin asked, surprised to see that Mrs. Martin had laid only one plate.

"I'll have mine later," she replied. "I've been so busy going over my accounts I reckon it's taken my mind off eating."

"Something wrong?" Orrin asked quickly.

"We'll get by," Mrs. Martin declared. "I'll watch expenses from here on." There was a tired look in her usually clear, expressive eyes. "It's right disappointing that all this had to happen."

She said no more, but in a way Orrin understood. Clara Martin's fixed purpose was to develop the dairy at Sunset Hill. This might already have been done if Blacky had worked with her kind of determination. But Clara often had to carry a double load, and progress was slowed. When Blacky had decided not to sell Golden Cloud, it had delayed Clara's plan to buy a highly bred bull. She had kept on saving without any complaint, only to be stopped again. And now, to make matters worse, there was the uncertainty about Blacky.

Sympathy for Clara Martin struck Orrin sharply. He remembered her wistfulness when she had spoken of the dress at Brown's and of her love of parties. He caught a glimpse of her face and saw the hurt look that she could not conceal. She made him think of a prisoner caught in a deep pit, who climbs laboriously toward the top, only to strike loose sand and then slide back.

Orrin stopped eating and stuck his fork into a tender square of ham, rolling it over on his plate. With a slow, sustained effort he swallowed the food that was in his mouth. The fork dropped back on the plate, with the morsel of ham pointing at the ceiling. His stomach had contracted until he felt as if he had gorged himself. Mrs. Martin's difficulties had become his own, with the added worry that only a boy can feel.

"Excuse me," he mumbled, pushing back the half-eaten breakfast. He rose and fumbled for the back door knob.

A heavy foot sounded on the back porch at that same time, and as Orrin stepped outside, Gabe Martin entered the kitchen.

Orrin's steps were aimless as he walked in the general direction of the barn. He scowled at the reddish dust billowing against the cloudless Oklahoma sky, and muttered at the monotony of the breeze on his cheeks and arms. Inside the barn he sank down on a bale of hay, his head resting heavily in his hands. He could not help noticing how far the supply of hay had dwindled. That reminded him that he was to start haying today, but for the time being he chose to ignore it. Absently he shredded some hay from a bale and pushed it around the barn floor with his toe. Right over there was where he had slept for a number of nights before Cloud had been born . . .

He rose and walked completely around the tractor. Close to the machine the smell of gasoline mingled with the savor of hay, producing a smell that was subtly pleasing to the boy . . . The doctors would probably set Blacky's broken bones today. He hoped there would be no complications. His parting words to Blacky about looking after things at the ranch returned to him, and this time he arose. There was just time enough to groom the palomino before Ike Johnson's man would arrive.

Orrin's hands were rough as he scoured Queen with the currycomb, and the mare flinched at the harsh handling of her head and ears. She grew restive under the silent manner of the boy, who usually talked so soothingly as he worked.

"O.K., now you're finished," Orrin growled, and

Queen's puzzled glance showed she could not understand the meaning of the boy's gruff manner.

He approached Golden Cloud in the same unceremonious way. But the filly pushed her nose under his arm and then looked at him with her head cocked so impudently that he had to grin.

"You little rascal," he crooned, with an arm around her neck, "you won't let me alone . . . Hey, young lady, you're beginning to fill out; you're growing up." He labored over Golden Cloud tenderly and felt better as he worked.

The wind had hardly drawn the dew from the grass when Ike Johnson's hired man Charley rode in on horseback. Behind him Tad followed bareback on his bay. The small boy's book bag and lunch box had been tied together with a long strap and slung across the horse's back.

"Hello, I haven't seen you in a long while," Orrin called to Tad. "Where have you been keeping yourself?"

"Went to the barber's yesterday," Tad grinned. "See?" He ran his hands above his ears where the hair had been closely clipped. It curved in a white rim against the tanned skin below. "Ma says there's no need to go to school today; the teacher won't know me."

"The barber did take a load off your mind at that," Orrin replied.

Charley, who was more than half Indian, good-natured and taciturn, dismounted in silence and motioned for Orrin to run the tractor out.

"How's Blacky getting along?" Tad called after Orrin. "I'm writing to Barbara about him. And how about the filly?"

Orrin paused. "Blacky broke his leg and collar bone. We think he's getting along O.K. And the filly—" A sudden weary, despondent feeling blurred his mind. What was the use of kidding himself? "—we're giving her to Gabe."

"I reckon he's tickled about that. She's a good-looker." Excited by this bit of news, Tad waved good-by, pulled his horse's head around, and continued on his way to school.

Charley, grunting patiently over the mower, hooked it to the tractor. "You drive," he told Orrin. He followed on horseback to the hayfield, where he watched Orrin manage it until he was satisfied the boy had the hang of it.

"Good. Good," Charley grunted; and Orrin, whose mind would not stay on his work, hardly noticed Charley leave.

Orrin stripped off his shirt and went methodically to work while the sun's rays bore down on his glistening back with ever-increasing heat. When he left the mower in the field and went to lunch, swath after swath of tall, fragrant grass lay ready for the rake.

"Did Gabe find you?" Mrs. Martin asked when she saw that he was alone.

He shook his head.

"I told him where you were, and he went out right after that . . . Come to think of it though, he didn't act quite like himself—no doubt thinking about Blacky."

"Probably," Orrin replied. They finished lunch, and after filling a milk bucket with drinking water, he returned to the fields.

At evening milking Orrin found Mrs. Martin in the cow barn, looking tired but cheerful. "I have good news about Blacky," she said. "He's coming home in a day or two, they think. They didn't find any internal injuries, thank the Lord. I asked the nurse to tell him that you are going ahead with the haying."

Halfway through supper, Gabe came in. He looked right past Orrin and refused Mrs. Martin's invitation to eat with them. Mrs. Martin told him eagerly about

Blacky's condition, but all Gabe said was, "Sure enough?" and went into the living room. Soon his loud snoring could be heard through the closed door.

After Orrin had washed the dishes, he said, "I left the tractor out; I'd better run it inside."

"I reckon I'll come along too, and take a look at that filly. Is she as smart as Blacky says she is?" The dishes in her hand rattled, otherwise she might have noticed that Orrin made no reply to her question.

Together they walked over the hill, Clara remarking about the good haying weather. While Orrin drove the tractor into the barn, she leaned against the rail fence of the paddock, watching Golden Cloud frisking about the other end. Her whistle brought the filly to a standstill, a marvel of symmetry and beauty.

"You whistle to her," she told Orrin when he stood beside her.

He obeyed and Cloud responded at a gallop.

"M-m-m," Mrs. Martin breathed appreciatively, "nice clean action—she's growing up as sound as a dollar and ten times as pretty. Gabe's chestnut filly yonder in the pasture sure looks ordinary after you've seen Cloud." She watched Orrin stroke the gracefully arched neck. "No wonder Gabe wants this one." And she added in a soft undertone, "It's a shame Blacky promised her to him."

Her words brought a hopeful surge to Orrin, but in the next moment his reason asserted itself. Mrs. Martin would never interfere with a promise made by her husband. After all, Cloud belonged to Blacky, and if he decided to give her away, it was his business. Besides, it would be three years before anything happened, wouldn't it?

"Things look a sight better around here since you've been with us," Mrs. Martin was saying. "You mended that rail fence yonder, didn't you? And you've cleaned up a lot of trash, too, along with working in the fields and at the dairy. I've sure come to depend on you, Orrin. And now I'll have to lean on you harder than ever."

"I've tried to do the best I could," he answered, and gave her an encouraging smile. She seemed smaller than usual in the dwindling light, and he knew that she really needed him. He felt strong and manly and important as he jumped over the paddock fence to lock up Cloud for the night.

The next morning Orrin was up and dressed before Mrs. Martin. He grinned to himself as he stole downstairs. She wouldn't have to be afraid that he would let her down when she was in a spot.

When his early chores took him to the stable, Orrin talked out loud steadily. "I've been doing a lot of thinking," he told Cloud. "You know, there are lots of ways in which this ranch could be improved. I never thought much about them before, but they're there. What about pasture?"

Golden Cloud looked inquiringly at Orrin with cocked head, and he interrupted himself to stroke her soft forehead.

"All we have to do is terrace those west fields and we can double our pasture. A lot of land around here has been terraced. No reason why we must have gullies all over the place. That's only one thing. All right, you want to know where the money's coming from. Well, Gabe gave me the idea. I'm going to be another Sonny Le May, only better, because you're going to be my trick horse."

Cloud accepted this verdict solemnly, but Orrin's eyes were gleaming. "I mean it, you overgrown jack rabbit. Two, three years from now you'll have a regular act. Think what that will mean to Mrs. Martin!"

The filly blinked, swished her short white tail, and turned to nuzzle Queen, who was no longer interested in what Orrin was saying.

"I've got things to do," he said when he hustled out. "Mrs. Martin is depending on me, but we'll have a little session for tricks later on."

A long, hard day in the fields loomed ahead of him. In the morning he rode the tractor while the side delivery rake kicked the cut hay into long windrows whose scent was lost in the smell of exhaust. After dinner he borrowed Mr. Johnson's baler and spent most of the afternoon baling hay. The session that he had promised Cloud was a scant quarter-hour squeeze in before he drove the cows from pasture.

At the end of the fifteen minutes he felt that he had accomplished nothing. Cloud would shake her head *no* when he tickled her ear, but a motion of his hand seemed to mean nothing. Most of the time was spent drawing her attention away from grasshoppers and birds and fluttering leaves.

"Sonny Le May said it takes patience," Orrin muttered when he had finished. "He wasn't kidding."

As if in reply, a short laugh floated across the paddock, and Orrin saw Gabe Martin coming toward him. Blacky's cousin idled up, excitement adding brilliance to his eyes and a trace of bluster to his voice. "You all having trouble with the parlor tricks?"

It was the first time Gabe had spoken to him since their quarrel at the Frontier Club. Orrin shrugged his shoulders. Gabe's drawling sarcasm angered him, but he replied quietly, "Plenty of time to train her, Gabe."

Orrin's mild reply seemed to strengthen Gab 's self-confidence. "Well," he said more loudly, "I'm surprised that Clara lets you waste your time with the palominos when there's a field full of hay waiting to be baled."

"There's no hay ready to be baled just now," Orrin replied quietly.

There was a sniff from Gabe and his glance shifted; meanwhile he muttered something about Yankee carpet-baggers. Aloud he grumbled, "The way this place is run doesn't make sense. I should have stayed in Texas where they have men to do the work."

"Texas hasn't moved lately," Orrin grunted as he watched Cloud dash across the turf. "It's still in the same place."

Gabe appeared undecided whether to act angry or amused. He took a step in Orrin's direction, hesitated, and forced a thin smile. "Listen, hired help, I've got me a lift back to Texas tomorrow morning, and a horse trailer for my little filly to ride in. Next time I move into the east bedroom there'll be nobody a-tall in the spare room. Adios, hired help, and take good care of the palomino for me."

As Gabe slid his legs over the paddock bars, Orrin scowled after him, wondering if he were really leaving. And if he did leave, did his threat mean anything?

9. Danger in the Paddock

ORRIN stood on a rise of ground adjoining the pecan grove and squinted into the sun's glare. He would not believe that Gabe was really leaving until he actually saw him go. A few steps behind Orrin, Clara Martin stood with her face turned in the same direction. Both of them were staring at a place where the highway emerged briefly from low, sun-browned hills to form a rounded black elbow.

The boy did not move until the top of a sedan slid into sight, followed by the upper half of a horse trailer. The sedan curved around the bend in the road, and for a moment both vehicles appeared in full view. A ray of early morning sunshine pointed at the open trailer and splashed against a filly's chestnut-colored back and head. Then Orrin nodded his head in satisfaction and turned around, giving a surprised start when he saw that Mrs. Martin was there also.

"He's gone," Clara said.

Orrin was not sure how she meant it. "It leaves us more shorthanded than ever," he replied.

"It's a good loss," Clara said with more sting in her voice than Orrin had ever heard. "He's plumb selfish, Orrin. He's done nothing but make more work for us—even after Blacky was hurt."

Orrin tried awkwardly to find something to say, but failed.

Mrs. Martin continued tartly, her left hand tightening at her side. "Wouldn't you think that a big, strapping fellow like Gabe would want to earn his keep? Five years ago he was winning big money at rodeos, and I sure thought he might amount to something. But he cracked a couple of ribs and gave it up. Now he says he's going into horse-breeding, and he keeps holding Blacky to his promise to look after him. . . . Not that I blame Blacky for always keeping his word. I respect him for it, Orrin. But Gabe will never change, and we have three more years to put up with him."

Slowly the scorn left Clara's eyes and a look of self-reproach took its place. She turned to Orrin and smiled wanly. "You won't repeat what I said, will you? I'll talk to Gabe the next time he comes back. Like as not he has his troubles too."

"I won't talk about it," he told her with sincerity. He had been impressed with Mrs. Martin's frankness and he felt drawn to her more closely than ever. Side by side they returned to the dairy, where each went thoughtfully about his own work.

A day at Sunset Hill was so crowded with things to do now that Orrin could hardly keep track of the time. The brush of wind against dry lips, the smell of the cow barn and stable, a swirl of reddish dust, and another day would pass.

Blacky remained at the hospital, and through necessity Orrin arranged his own daily work. As he went from one job to another, endless plans for the ranch rushed through his mind, thoughts that seemed to drive his hands faster in their work. Woven into his ideas to terrace fields or rotate crops or remodel buildings, one thread remained constant, and that was his determination to teach Golden Cloud a routine of tricks. Not a day went by that he did not spend at least a few minutes with the palomino. That daily lesson and the evening talk with Clara Martin about the next day's work gave Orrin a feeling of contentment he had not experienced since he was a small child.

Blacky's absence did not depress him, except as it was a cause of worry for Clara. Each time she visited the hospital she reported on Blacky's condition; and although she talked little about him otherwise, his slow recovery troubled her.

When Clara finally brought home the news that Blacky would soon be returning, she immediately began to plan for his home-coming.

"We're too busy to invite anyone else," she told Orrin, "but we'll have to have a party for Blacky—just you and he and I, but we'll pretend there's a crowd of us. Might make him feel better if he knows we aren't worrying." With the back of a knife she began to spread a coating of chocolate icing over a sponge cake. For a minute she stared out the kitchen window, and the knife, still stroking back and forth, pushed bare a strip across the top of the cake. "It does seem queer," she mused, "they didn't send him home sooner . . . I wonder . . ."

Orrin tried to make himself look forward to Blacky's arrival. He took pains to move the rancher's bed nearer to the window, where he would be able to look past the paddocks and watch Queen. Clara Martin's smile at this thoughtfulness was more than enough reward for Orrin.

Long before the ambulance arrived within sight, Clara and Orrin had caught the whine of its siren. They were waiting at the front door when it drew up to the house. Two men lifted Blacky's stretcher out and followed Mrs. Martin to the house.

"He looks as fat and sassy as a big old jay bird," Mrs. Martin told the men; but Orrin was startled by the sallow color of his face. The grin that answered Clara's remark was tired and forced.

"Lands," Clara said cheerfully to Blacky as the stretcher bearers went up the stairs, "you're wrapped up in enough bandages to cover a house. And your hair! It needed cutting before you got thrown, now it's hiding your collar. I'll trim it before I do another thing."

Following a step behind Mrs. Martin, Orrin listened to her voice and felt uneasily that she was trying to hide an unaccustomed nervousness.

The men lifted Blacky into bed. They adjusted the pillows, talked a moment to Mrs. Martin and left.

Orrin now had his first chance to talk to Blacky. "Feel good to be home?"

The ranchman nodded slowly. He shifted in bed to get a clearer view of his ranch, but the movement made him wince, and the lines deepened at the corners of his mouth.

"Now then," Clara smiled, bustling toward him with a pair of scissors and a towel, "I'm going to see if I've forgotten how to shear wool." Working the scissors in her left hand, Mrs. Martin cut and snipped deftly until a pile of coarse black hair lay on the white towel. "I reckon it won't quite make a bale," she teased when she stopped cutting and shook the loose hair into a waste-basket.

Blacky, after enduring the haircut patiently, looked at Orrin in his old, quizzical way. "With the scalp lock Clara's left me, I'd pass for Kiowa Joe's blood brother."

"You're not heading for the warpath," Mrs. Martin laughed. "The three of us are going to make good medicine with a home-coming party."

Blacky seemed to enter into the spirit of the occasion, offering a dry remark from time to time. But after the cake had been served and Mrs. Martin had cleared away the crumbs, his eyes closed and his fingers relaxed.

She motioned to Orrin and together they quietly left the room.

The next day Blacky seemed more at ease, but his color was no better. His cheeks had lost the glow and vigor of stout saddle leather. Orrin looked away from him much of the time while he talked about the ranch. "The kafir corn's doing fine, hay's all baled and stacked, and I've caught up on some of the odd jobs," he said proudly. He hesitated a moment, then decided to mention what was in his mind. "I've been teaching Cloud how to shake her head *no*, and she's catching on. She'll kneel now if I just touch one knee."

To Orrin's disappointment, Blacky showed no interest in this fact. "Heard anything from Gabe?" he asked, and Orrin shook his head.

Another time he tried to talk to Blacky about his ideas for improving the ranch. "Couldn't we terrace some of the land that's going to waste and put it into wheat pasture?"

But Blacky did not react to Orrin's new feeling of re-sponsibility for the future of the ranch. "That would take money," he said, as if that settled it. "We couldn't make a go of it."

Orrin walked away gloomily from Blacky's bed, realizing that after all he was only a hired hand and not a partner. After this conversation it seemed to him that Blacky became annoyed every time they were together without Clara; and the boy talked no more of building up the ranch.

Late one afternoon Orrin found himself with nothing that demanded immediate attention. The corn had grown too tall to need cultivation, the barn was stuffed with bales of pale green hay, and additional bales lay piled in the field under tarpaulins. He was using his time to build a small inclosure adjoining the paddock, which he had told Cloud would be her schoolroom. He swung the gate a few times to test the fit when he heard a boy's sharp voice calling, "Hey, Orrin."

"Hi!" Orrin shouted back to Tad Johnson, who had ridden up bareback and was now looking down into the paddock. "Come over here and take a look."

"Can't," Tad said importantly. "I've got to find Mrs. Martin."

"Did you try the house?"

"She's not there."

Orrin barred his new gate and crossed the paddock, Cloud trotting along curiously behind him. He turned and fondled the filly's head with both hands while he talked to Tad. "Maybe she's up at the cow barn. It's a little early, but she might be there. We'll go and see."

Tad slid to the ground and threw his horse's reins over the paddock gate post. "What are you building?" he asked as they started up the hill.

"A training corral for Cloud."

Tad gave the filly an approving look. "She's sure coming along good, but she's too young to train. She isn't old enough to wean yet."

"It'll surprise you how much they can learn when they

113

are young," Orrin asserted with the air of a veteran trainer. "There's a ranch where they raise albinos, and they have them fully trained when they are two-year-olds."

Tad looked at Orrin again to make sure he was serious. "Barbara's coming home for the summer in a couple of weeks. Wait till I tell her that."

"There might be a few things about horses that she doesn't know," Orrin observed testily.

Tad shrugged his shoulders and hurried along without debating the point.

The big doors at either end of the cow barn were wide open, and to Orrin's surprise the cows were already in their stanchions. At the far end of the barn Mrs. Martin was pushing fresh hay to each cow with a pitchfork.

"Daddy sent me over to ask a favor, Mrs. Martin," Tad called as he walked past the row of swishing tails. "The county man is helping him dig a new pond and our tractor broke down."

"And you want to borrow ours," Mrs. Martin added smiling.

"Daddy'd like to borrow yours," Tad continued, as if he had thought out the words in advance and must say them this way. "They can finish the job before dark with it."

"Glad to do anything for you," Clara agreed heartily. "It sure seems like we're always borrowing something from your father."

"I'll go tell him," Tad said, "and I sure thank you."

"Hurry back," Mrs. Martin called as the boy left. She leaned on the pitchfork and spoke to Orrin. "You run along with the tractor and I'll follow with the pickup to bring you back. Milking can wait; the cows came in early this evening."

"How come?"

Mrs. Martin looked reflectively at the nearest cow.

"That big old dog of Caldwell's was snooping around the place until I chased him home. I reckon he scared the cattle and started them on the move. But they've quieted down now, and they will be right happy to eat their hay until we get back."

"I'll get going then," Orrin said. "See you over there."

Shortly the tractor was bowling along the edge of the highway, and Orrin, perched behind the wheel, looked the part of a sturdy, native Oklahoman instead of a city lad.

Tad was waiting in front of his house to direct the tractor through a pasture gate. Down the slope Orrin could see a bulldozer ramming against a pile of earth, and off to one side he could see Ike Johnson bustling about with another man.

Ike paused long enough to shake the perspiration from his face and to thank Orrin for the tractor. Then he hooked a steel scoop behind the tractor, and soon its clamor joined the roar of the bulldozer as the men hurried to finish their work before dark.

It was Orrin's first opportunity to observe a major improvement of this kind. He stood back where he could see the excavation deepen and take shape, and it excited him. There was reality in the work going on before him. Projects such as this could be planned and carried out at Sunset Hill, no matter what Blacky thought.

He was hardly aware that Mrs. Martin was at his side now, and that she too was fascinated by the intense activity below them. Conversation would have been difficult amid the constant pounding of machines, but neither made any attempt to talk. They watched much longer than they should, for each felt keenly the parallel between this digging of Ike Johnson's pond and the many improvements that should be made at Sunset Hill Ranch.

Upstairs in his bedroom Blacky Martin had listened to the clatter of the tractor recede down the drive when Orrin had taken it out. Then Clara had called to him to say she was driving over to Johnsons to pick up Orrin. Blacky shifted his weight laboriously and tried to settle himself for a nap. The intense heat that seeped through the walls of his room made him drowsy, but he was unable to sleep.

A fly buzzed around the room until Blacky caught it with a crafty swoop of his free hand as it flew near him. He was wide awake now. For a time his mind dwelt on his injury and the extra expense and inconvenience it had caused. He thought of how the setback had hurt Clara's plans, and it seemed to deepen the pain that lay dully in his chest. Sliding his hand resolutely over the edge of the bed, he fumbled in the drawer of the small table that held his personal articles. He pulled out a book that showed little trace of wear, called *The Business of Ranching*.

Clara had given it to him as a Christmas present the first year they were married. He had never managed to get any information from its pages, but he attacked it now with fierce determination, as if he hoped to learn something that would help him pay for the damage his accident had caused.

Blacky's forehead puckered over the book and his lips moved with the print until the letters wavered back and forth and then faded away. "It's no use," he muttered, "I can rope these words, but I can't get the pickin' string on them." He pondered a while. "I could lend the book to Orrin. He's young and smart and full of ideas—he'll understand it."

Some of the ideas Orrin had offered came back to Blacky as he glanced out the window. In his mind he could see terraced fields green with corn and alfalfa as

Orrin had pictured them. He knew it could be done; he knew that he should fall in with Orrin's plans instead of stubbornly resisting them. The agricultural agent had outlined the preliminary steps, but somehow whenever it had been possible to use terracing equipment, Blacky had been at the Frontier Club breaking in one of his horses. Now his pride prevented him from accepting suggestions that he knew would work.

Blacky drew as deep a breath as his injuries would permit, and turned his head for a glimpse of Queen in the pasture beyond the paddock. Although his second-story window gave him almost full view of the field, he could not locate her. In sudden fear that thieves were on the loose again while he was alone on the ranch, he tried to raise himself higher.

Another look, while he forced himself to remain calm, and his hand dropped back on the bed in relief. There was Queen over against the paddock fence, standing near the filly, who was inside the paddock. As expert on horses as he was, Blacky delighted in studying the lines and color of the dam and her foal.

But what was happening out there now? Queen had suddenly thrown up her head and Blacky could hear her angry cry as she backed away from the fence. The filly, too, suddenly pulled back her ears and whirled in panic. With a shrill snort of fear she bolted out of sight toward the barn.

There was danger abroad in the paddock and Blacky could not get down there to find out what it was! Could it be fire? He sniffed for the rank odor of burning hay, but there were no traces of smoke. Had a thief crept into the paddock with an eye on the filly? Blacky thought of his shotgun in his bedroom closet, but just the quick tensing of his muscles brought dots of perspiration to his forehead.

Queen was now dashing wildly along her side of the fence in a frenzy, snorting angrily.

"Something must be after the filly, and Queen wants to get to her," Blacky groaned to himself. He shouted through the open window, "Back up, Queen, and jump that fence!" but his voice was lost in the strong breeze.

Once again the filly galloped into sight, squealing for Queen's help. And then a cry carried deep and fierce to Blacky as Caldwell's huge dog leaped at the filly's heels.

Finding no aid from her mother, Cloud wheeled on her slim hind legs and lashed out with her forefeet. For a moment Blacky forgot the danger the horse was in, and his eyes gleamed with admiration for the palomino's courage, but the dog leaped out of range and kept worrying her with his savage yelping. In desperation, Golden Cloud flashed away in a burst of speed—the best protection that nature had given her.

"That dog is sure loco," Blacky muttered as he saw the ugly beast lurch in pursuit. "He must have nicked the filly somewhere and caught the taste of blood. If he doesn't kill her, he's going to cripple her." Blacky's feeling of helplessness made him strain like an unbroken horse against a rope. "Get out of there!" he screamed as the dog trailed Cloud in Queen's direction. Not even an echo followed the outburst.

The paddock fence made straightaway escape impossible, and the predicament of the filly was growing rapidly worse. With his killer's instinct telling him that it was nearly time to close in for the kill, the dog pressed his advantage and was growing bolder with each jump.

Blacky pictured the body of a magnificent filly lying mutilated in the paddock, and he remembered his promise to Gabe. But the pain in his chest held him in bed. Then he thought of Orrin and how Golden Cloud worshiped him—saw in his mind the boy's unbelieving stare as he leaned over a golden form spattered with red.

Slowly Blacky managed to prop himself to his elbows; he then slid his sound leg over the side of the bed until his foot met the floor. He stopped to catch his breath and fight the weight that pressed against his lungs. His good knee cushioned the fall of his broken leg as he sank to the floor.

The sudden exertion and the pain drove a gray wall before Blacky's eyes. His head dropped weakly, but it permitted the circulation of blood to climb back to his brain. The courage and determination that had made him top man at many a rodeo gave him strength to start inching along the floor toward the closet.

"Keep fanning—keep fighting," he muttered, but whether he was speaking to himself or to the harassed Cloud, he wouldn't have known himself.

Time that he could not estimate passed until his hand, damp with sweat, pulled the shotgun from its corner. Another endless struggle until the hot breeze blew through the open window upon his face. Little by little he worked his fingers until he loosened the catch on the screen and felt it swing outward. Then the barrel of the gun grated across the window sill and pointed toward the Paddock.

The agony in Blacky's chest was intense; muscles like rawhide plaits stood out along the column of his neck. His breath was coming in jerky gasps when his right eye finally peered down the matted rib of the gun.

A victorious roar from Caldwell's dog sounded from below the hill, and Blacky felt himself start to go limp, for he was afraid it was too late. Suddenly his eyes focused on a gleaming creature that hobbled into view, dragging a shape that clung to her hind leg. It was Golden Cloud, stumbling on, the dog's teeth searching for the hamstring.

There was still a chance; Blacky fought to remain conscious. Desperately he looked down the barrel. At this distance it would be better to fire over the heads of the two animals in the hope of frightening the dog by the gun's explosion.

Golden Cloud demonstrated once more the courage that had been bred into her through her Arabian sire and the gallant Queen. Muscles that had been toughening in daily play gathered for one last effort. They constricted swiftly, and her hind legs drove against that fearful weight.

The suddenness of the lunge caught the dog by surprise. With a sharp howl he was flung loose, thrown off balance for the moment, but not really hurt. The filly staggered on, and the dog, more furious than ever, bounded in pursuit.

At this moment Blacky squeezed the trigger of the shotgun. The blast drove the weakened rancher backward, and the gun, with a thin wisp of smoke curling from the muzzle, teetered on the window sill before plunging to the ground.

The pickup carrying Mrs. Martin and Orrin was rounding the driveway when Orrin asked, "Did you hear something that sounded like a gun?"

Mrs. Martin nodded, her eyes grave for a moment. Then she said practically, "Maybe somebody in a tractor is stopping by." Nevertheless, her foot settled down more firmly on the accelerator.

"Look!" she cried an instant later, "that's Caldwell's dog over there. I thought I chased him away." The huge animal, with tail drooping, was legging it through the pecan grove.

Instead of driving past the house, Mrs. Martin stopped in front of it. She laughed shortly as if ashamed of herself for making such a suggestion. "Run in and see if Blacky is asleep," she said.

Orrin sensed an air of anxiety in the quiet of the house as he hurried through the kitchen. He laughed nervously on the way upstairs, and would have shouted to Blacky as he ran, just to relieve the silence, only it would have been silly to interrupt Blacky's nap.

Orrin's face lighted with a tense smile of greeting as he poked his head into Blacky's room. At sight of the empty bed the smile left his face. Two more quick strides brought him in view of Blacky's slumping figure. Two more, and he was kneeling at Blacky's side, dropping his head to the rancher's chest to listen for his heart. Orrin was not sure, so he rolled back an eyelid and thought he noticed signs of life. Tenderly he eased the limp body into a more comfortable position. Then he dashed down the steps to tell Mrs. Martin.

Clara Martin's left hand gripped the steering wheel hard when she saw the look in Orrin's eyes. She interrupted him before he could tell her the whole story. "You go phone for a doctor while I run upstairs."

The pickup shook as Orrin jumped behind the wheel and stepped on the gas. As he drove, he frowned over the cause of Blacky's accident, wondering if Cloud could have been involved in any way.

In a few minutes Orrin was back. He ran to Blacky's room where Clara, steady-eyed and efficient, was gently pressing a cool, damp cloth on his forehead. "Doctor Hartung is coming," he told her. "He said he'd hurry. Blacky's still—out?"

"He moved his head once and sort of grunted. I reckon he's collecting his strength to tell us what happened."

Orrin looked at the slack form on the floor. Blacky's hands appeared small and frail against his pajamas; his shoulders seemed thinner. But somehow in his face, perhaps in the set of his mouth, there clung a suggestion of rugged integrity, the toughness that was Blacky Martin's.

"You can't keep old Blacky down," Orrin mused. "You've got to admire the guy for it."

But he had not yet found out about Cloud. With a quick movement he stepped past Blacky, and looked out the window, where, in one sweeping glance, he could examine the pasture.

Queen was gone! Orrin knew he had left her in full view of Blacky's window. His hands were clammy as he looked next toward the paddock for Cloud. He squinted in wonderment at what he saw. There was Queen on the wrong side of the fence, running her tongue over the filly, who was crowding close to her mother's flank. But what had made the mare jump the fence?

A new voice sounded in the bedroom, and Dr. Hartung, somewhat out of breath, started to talk. There was impatience in his tone, and Orrin, blinking at him stupidly, finally realized that the doctor wanted him to help lift Blacky back into the bed.

"He'll come around pretty soon," he heard Dr. Hartung say. "The cast on his leg seems all right, but I'm afraid there is trouble up here." His fingers pressed lightly against the adhesive tape that covered Blacky's chest and shoulder. "Now why in the world would a man in his condition want to get out of—"

A groan from Blacky interrupted him and then the lips began to move. "Doc Rawlings," Blacky gasped weakly.

The doctor's eyebrows raised.

"Has he been delirious?"

Blacky seemed to hear and managed to say, "Filly . . ." before the effort overcame him.

Orrin glanced toward the window, but Dr. Hartung was talking, explaining how Blacky should be cared for until he sent an ambulance.

Before the doctor left, Blacky managed to pant out the story. Dr. Hartung pursed his lips and shook his head in reproof. "You never should have done that just for a horse."

A spark of indignation jumped to Blacky's dark eyes and Orrin caught the words as Blacky said jerkily, "Just a horse? That little palomino! Ask Orrin . . ."

Dr. Hartung looked over his glasses at Orrin. but the boy was already on the move.

"I'm going to Cloud," he called back as he ran from the room.

10. Outlaw Horses

ORRIN took the shortest route to the paddock, down the hill and over the fence. When he was fifty yards away, he could see a blotch above Cloud's hock; and coming closer, he saw the ugly pink furrows in the matted hair.

Golden Cloud started nervously at the sound of his approach and tried to hobble away and hide behind Queen. But when she heard Orrin's voice and felt his hand on her head, her trembling lessened.

"All right, Cloud. All right. Take it easy." Orrin's first worry was that there might be disfiguring scars, but then he realized there could be worse dangers. The best thing to do was to run back and tell Mrs. Martin.

Mrs. Martin looked up, tightly calm, as Orrin described the injuries. "You run right down and get Doc Rawlings.

Blacky has to go back to the hospital, but there's nothing you can do for him." She waved him out. "Go ahead."

When Orrin reached Doc Rawlings' house, the vet himself came to the door. He complained that the call was inconvenient, coming at supper time, but nevertheless he jumped into the pickup behind Orrin.

"Do you think there is danger of infection?" Orrin asked anxiously.

Doc Rawlings growled something, but did not see fit to answer the question until he had seen the nature of the wounds. When presently he knelt in the box stall beside the filly, he grunted to himself with such a deep furrowing of his forehead that Orrin asked him the same question again.

The vet reached for his bag and indicated that he did not like to be questioned while he worked. "First things first," he growled as he prepared to give Cloud a shot.

Orrin's eyes blinked at the amount of fluid to be injected. While the boy held Cloud's head, Doc Rawlings gave a quick stab with the needle. Orrin flinched, but Cloud gave only one slight shudder. Doc Rawlings was pleased. "She's a good one!" he muttered.

After he had bound up the deeper gashes and painted the small ones, the vet's seamy face eased. "There," he said, "after she gets over the effects of that shot, she'll be fit again. And young as she is, she'll just naturally outgrow any scars that might show at first. I'll drop in again tomorrow and take a look at her. . . . What excuse did old Caldwell give for not keeping his dog chained?"

"I haven't talked to him."

"Well, somebody should. That dog has already chewed up two good heifers. He ought to be done away with."

After he had taken the doctor back to his home, Orrin wanted to stay in the stall with Cloud and talk to her, but he had to find Mrs. Martin.

Her renewed anxiety over Blacky had not kept Clara from her work however. She was at the cow barn, and she stopped milking to ask Orrin, "How is Golden Cloud?"

"She's all treated. Doc Rawlings thinks she'll be as good as ever. But what about Blacky?"

"I'm to call up later. The ambulance came while you were gone." An almost continuous river of milk splashed into the milk bucket under her left hand. When she paused, her eyes seemed clearer. "Perhaps it's all for the best. Blacky was doing poorly before. Maybe they'll find the seat of the trouble this time."

Orrin really shared the hope that Blacky's latest injuries would lead to a fresh start toward recovery. But he already had the feeling that again he was in partnership with Mrs. Martin in sketching the daily pattern of ranch life.

Clara's black-covered account book was kept close at hand in the days that followed, and she studied it with an absorbed frown. Uneasily Orrin would glance at her and then plan harder to find additional leisure to teach Cloud, as if in this way he could shorten the time until the filly's talents could be turned into money.

The day Clara Martin received Doc Rawlings' bill, Orrin realized how serious their situation was. "Twenty bucks is worth saving," he reflected. "Somebody should have gone to Old Man Caldwell right away and kicked up a fuss about his dog. He ought to consider himself lucky if I let him off by merely having him pay the bill."

When Orrin told Clara what he intended to do, she gave him a peculiar look. "I meant to talk turkey to Bill Caldwell the day Cloud was hurt, but I wasn't up to it—and I've been making excuses to myself ever since. You try, Orrin, if you've a mind to; but don't be disappointed if he gets the best of you."

"We'll see," Orrin said, reacting to Mrs. Martin's tired

glance with a determination to fight for her. "I'll go right now while I'm in the mood."

With the vet's bill in his shirt pocket, Orrin drove up to the Caldwell farm.

In answer to Orrin's knock, a big man in suspenders and shirt sleeves stepped outside. "Hello, there," he called cordially. His blue eyes twinkled under a lick of white hair, and his round face spread in genial lines. "What can I do for you?"

"I am afraid my reason for dropping in isn't pleasant, Mr. Caldwell."

"How's that? I can't hear you. You say it's a pleasant day?"

Orrin stepped closer and tried again. He raised his voice. "I came to see you about your dog."

"My dog? Yes, sir, he's right here in the kitchen. Tug, come here."

An enormous dog with sullen eyes limped to the screen door. "Look at the poor feller," Mr. Caldwell said wrathfully. "Somebody pumped him half full of buckshot t'other day." Caldwell's eyes gleamed like blue agate. "I'll have to chain him up now to keep him from being molested."

Orrin felt his determination weaken under Caldwell's fierce manner, but he looked the man right in the eye as he handed him Doc Rawlings' bill.

Mr. Caldwell's glance seemed to penetrate right through the billhead. "Course it's too high," he growled. "Young feller, don't pay a penny more than ten dollars. If it was me, I wouldn't have Doc Rawlings; Darrow's a heap more reasonable." Mr. Caldwell reached toward the screen door, his blue eyes friendly again. "Stop in some time when I'm not so busy," he said heartily.

Confused, Orrin realized that he had not even made any direct accusation against the dog, but he felt so completely on the defensive that he could not decide how to begin now. Mr. Caldwell had turned his back and was singing as he puttered with a window. Orrin shook his head helplessly, and with a few uncomplimentary thoughts about himself and Mr. Caldwell, he started glumly back to tell Mrs. Martin about his failure.

On two different occasions after this visit, Orrin sat down and composed letters to Mr. Caldwell asking him to pay the vet's bill, but neither one was ever mailed. The matter ended when Clara sent Doc Rawlings twenty dollars and received in return a receipted bill.

When Blacky came home from the hospital the second time, he no longer acted depressed. "My chest is healing right this time," he said with conviction after he had lain in his bed for a few days. "They called in specialists and I can feel the difference already. I reckon it was a good thing I cracked that bone again."

"Specialists," Clara Martin echoed under her breath. She knew what kind of bill that would add up to.

That night they had black-eyed peas for supper, and Mrs. Martin apologized for not serving a dessert. But later in the evening this was forgotten when several men from the Frontier Club, who had been tacking up rodeo posters along the highway, stopped in to see Blacky.

Orrin sat down with the visitors, enjoying the drawling stories and quiet chuckles and the way they accepted him as a member of the ranch family. Blacky joked about competing in the rodeo, saying he would try for the prize in the novices' bronc-riding contest. The men pretended to take him seriously.

"The shape you're in," one of them said, "you better stay out of the novice class. They'll be clawing each other like locoed grizzlies to get that three hundred bucks. Biggest single prize in the show."

"How come?" Blacky asked.

"Sim Remy got some big dude store in the city to kick in the money. I reckon they think it's good advertising."

Blacky sighed. "I'd sure like to get into that contest . . . Reminds me of the rodeo at Calgary in Alberta, Canada, when I figured I had a sure thing in the steer riding." And thus the story-swapping continued.

When Orrin went for the mail in the morning he found one of the rodeo posters hanging from the mailbox. Two more gave gaudy dabs of color to the cottonwood tree across the road. "I'll take this one off the mailbox and hang it up in Blacky's room. He'll get a kick out of seeing it," he thought to himself.

But Blacky did not respond to the poster the way Orrin had expected. He was in a more serious frame of mind than he had been the night before. His expression now was actually downcast, and it seemed to hurt him to look at the poster. "I been kind of thinking of selling old Buck," he said to Orrin.

"Your roping pony!"

Blacky's stubby forefinger smothered a wrinkle in his sheet. "Keeping him is plumb luxury," he said. "What do I want with a little old buckskin?"

Orrin shifted his gaze, for he knew that in Blacky's eyes the buckskin was as much a fixture on the ranch as the red barn.

"I won't be riding for a good long spell," Blacky mused, "and old Buck is too much trouble to keep around any longer. Time somebody got stuck with him besides me."

Just how much trouble Buck caused, Orrin understood well. Out in all kinds of weather and capable of living on the barest forage, the range-bred animal could be forgotten for months on end. "You can't get rid of Buck," Orrin protested.

"Tell that to Clara, hear?" Blacky said half seriously as

Orrin walked away, still carrying the bright piece of cardboard.

He stopped at his own room and tossed the poster on his bed. It landed right side up, the vivid letters boasting of star attractions and big prize money. "If only I had Gabe's ability," he thought, "prize money like this would be easy picking. You can bet I wouldn't let myself slip the way he did . . ."

Off and on during the day he thought about the rodeo until the sudden expanding of an idea aroused him. "I'm certainly a novice," he thought, "but that doesn't say I haven't a chance to win the three hundred bucks." He was trying to test his idea cautiously, but already a feeling of excitement was stirring in his chest. "It wouldn't be any worse than the time I jumped Ripple," he argued to himself, "and now I know more about riding."

The challenge to ride in the rodeo carried such a fascination of danger that Orrin could not keep it out of his mind. He could see himself handing three hundred dollars to Clara Martin with the easy remark, "Here's a little something I picked up on the side." And at Clara's protests, he would smile and say, "You and I are partners and that's the way I want to do this." That thought was enough to make him feel important to Sunset Hill Ranch, even though Blacky was home again.

There were times, however, when he could not help but give way to pessimism. Supposing he were thrown and injured badly. It had happened to a horseman as expert as Blacky, and he had only been riding a green stock horse.

Orrin leaned against the paddock fence and talked to Cloud about it. "I wouldn't mind losing, Cloud, or being banged up; but if I landed in the hospital . . ." It made him sweat to think what that would mean, but after a bit he continued, "Then again, there's always the chance I

130

might win. Three hundred dollars would really be a shot in the arm for Mrs. Martin right now."

Golden Cloud showed mild curiosity in his conversation. Her ears, like delicate golden shells, pointed first forward and then back. She laid her muzzle across the fence so that her master could fondle her as he talked.

"If I decide to enter," Orrin went on, "it's really your fault. Blacky got hurt protecting you, you know."

A rabbit hopped between the rails and gave Cloud a saucy look. Inquisitively the filly took a few steps and bent her head down to make friends, but in a moment she forgot everything except the urge to stretch her muscles in a carefree run around the paddock.

Orrin watched the play of Cloud's hind legs. The wounds no longer bothered her, and there seemed to be no stiffness or pain in her stride. "We haven't had hard luck all the time," he reflected, thinking of her quick recovery, "maybe that's a sign that I should enter the rodeo."

When he asked Blacky if it would be all right to ride Buck, the rancher chuckled. "Ride him as often as you like. He'll be getting a hay belly loafing around here. You won't find him as smooth riding as old Ripple, but he'll sure take you where you're going."

"I want to get used to riding different horses," Orrin explained. He did not say that he intended to ride Buck without a saddle. That would have led to questions he preferred not to answer.

As the opening day of the rodeo approached, he pretended in his own mind that he was still balancing the risks of competition against the long chance of winning. Actually he knew that he would feel cowardly if he gave up the rodeo idea. He even knew that his excuse for leaving the ranch would be to look up some books on horse-training at the city library, a plausible reason, because he had been talking about the books for a long time.

Neither Blacky nor Clara was the least bit surprised one morning when Orrin hustled through his work in order to have the afternoon free to go to the library. And if they saw Orrin with his hands in Cloud's white mane when he bade her good-by, they were too far away to know that this farewell was any different from usual.

The woman in the library may have thought Orrin acted absentminded, but she made no comment at first. But when he picked up the wrong book, she shook her head. "I'm afraid you are wool-gathering," she said.

Orrin gave her a blank look, fumbled for the right book, and mumbled, "Yes, ma'am," as he hurried away.

His thoughts continued to shut him off from all outside distractions until he saw the arrow that pointed to the Frontier Club. The arrow's tip slanted downward, and it suddenly loomed before Orrin like a symbol leading to ruin. Following this arrow had caused Blacky's failure, and now Orrin was turning off the main highway in the same direction.

When the pickup reached the board fence, Orrin could hear the rumble that swelled from a profusion of sounds. "There seems to be a big crowd here already," he muttered.

He stood hesitantly beside the pickup until a brassy tune shrilled from the band. The piece ended with a flourish, and a trumpeter blew a fanfare. A voice over a public address system announced: "Ladies and gentlemen—the grand entry of the cow girls and cowboys!"

To the accompaniment of yippees, a file of brightly dressed men and women on horseback thundered around the arena. Orrin could see their brilliant pennants flash past.

Excitement seethed in the grandstand as the announcer cried, "The next event is the men's bronc riding.

For this contest we have assembled the Southwest's most vicious outlaws—"

Without hesitating any longer, Orrin strode to the box office and paid his admission. Once inside the gate, he worked his way through a thicket of arms and legs to find breathing room farther down the side line.

When he turned around and stood on his toes he could see the first wild bronc rider on top of chute No. 1, watching closely for his chance to climb on the horse's back.

The announcer took advantage of this moment to add to the excitement. His voice was dramatically low: "Climbing aboard the hurricane deck of these range outlaws makes lion taming a parlor sport. These horses know no masters. They are the wild, unbroken lawlessness of the old West. When Kansas Twister comes roaring out with his human freight, you will see a battle—"

"Yow-hooo!" somebody screamed as a bucking, twisting demon leaped into the arena. His rider was gamely "dusting" the bronc with his hat, while his body bent one way and his head jerked in another.

"Ride 'em!" shrieked the fans as the bronc reared and pitched.

"O-o-o-o!" The groan was universal as the rider suddenly flew into the air, arms and legs asprawl.

The cowboy lay in a heap on the ground, his hands over his head, while the bronc, still bucking, flailed his hoofs dangerously close.

Two officials, skilled at the business, closed on the bucker and loosened the bucking strap. The rider limped back to join the other contestants in front of the chutes.

"And that was a good ride!" cried the announcer. "Now in chute No. 3 our next cowboy will make his bid on Black Satan."

The event continued, only one man staying on top until the pickup men lifted him off. At the conclusion of the bronc riding the announcer declared: "Winner of today's first prize money is Pete Boulder, for his ride on Storm Warning. Before we continue with the cow girls' event, I wish to call your attention to the bareback riding contest for novices. Oklahoma's leading tack shop has donated two hundred and fifty dollars in prize money for this event. The directors of this rodeo are adding another fifty dollars to make this an outstanding event to encourage new talent . . . And here's a friendly tip. If you want the best hand-tooled saddle in the Southwest at the lowest price, you'll find it at Lawson's."

Orrin's attention shifted to the conversation of two men in front of him. "Go ahead and enter," one said. "They don't use outlaws for novices. They're just little old ponies that don't know much about bucking."

A vivid image of cowboys diving from the tops of bucking broncs came to Orrin's mind. He wondered if the man was a practical joker. But all along Orrin had been dominated by one idea, so he pushed hurriedly to the edge of the arena and called to a judge:

"Where do I enter the novices' bareback riding?"

The judge pointed to the platform above the chutes and answered laconically, "Yonder."

A plump-faced woman wearing a cowboy hat tied under her chin took Orrin's name. She patted him on the arm and said archly, "Don't let them throw you, *Vaquero*."

"I'll try not to," Orrin replied, hoping he looked confident and reckless. "What kind of nags are they going to put us on?"

"Oh, you," she laughed reprovingly. "You mustn't call them nags. They're real broncos—*mucho* ornery. Ten dollars entry fee, please; and be back here five minutes before the event—*Sir?*"

"Ten—ten dollars?" Orrin gulped. He laid eight one-dollars bills on the table, added some silver and followed its course wistfully as the woman swept it into a drawer.

Five minutes before the novices' event, Orrin joined a group of twelve uneasy young men, all of whom were attempting to hide their fears in various ways.

"It doesn't worry me," one of them boasted. "I've been riding half-broke horses all my life."

A perspiring judge drawled out the instructions. Then they drew slips of paper giving the order in which they would ride. Orrin held his in his hand for a moment, and then slowly turned it over.

"Contestant No. 7—chute No. 3—on Sleepy Sam," Orrin read.

A boy of Orrin's age, who had drawn ride number six, crumpled his paper suddenly and threw it to the ground. He slouched away, shaking his head and muttering. Two others looked solemnly at each other and then walked off together, laughing nervously.

The other nine stood firm, no doubt sharing Orrin's thought that their chances of winning were just that much better.

The first three contestants climbed to the tops of their chutes, ready to take their turns.

"It's Smokestack coming out of chute No. 2," the announcer spoke into the microphone above Orrin's head. "And the first man in the novice event, Jim Tremaine, will show us how to ride him. Good luck Jim . . . Judges, stand by in case of injuries."

Orrin exchanged glances with his competitors at this warning. Hastily they drew away from chute No. 2 as a heavy body rocked the boards inside. Then Jim

135

Tremaine was on the horse's back and the gate swung open.

That rider had no chance of staying on Smokestack, for the powerful animal bounded into the arena as if running away, jarred to a sudden halt with head down, and rider No. 1 was disposed of in exactly three-tenths of a second. Orrin winced at the dull thump of the man's body on the ground. But Tremaine picked himself up and walked back in a dazed curve. "I sure thought we were going to reach Arizona in time for supper," he said with a sickly smile.

Within the chutes the horses squealed and whinnied and shook the stout timbers. One after another they plunged into the arena. Shortly thereafter would follow a quick impression of a man's body jerking and bouncing until his head snapped back and his heels flew up. A quick gasp would come from the crowd, the thump of the contestant's body; and a riderless horse would go kicking down the arena.

Soon Orrin felt himself grip the ladder to the top of chute No. 3 with a detached feeling that it was someone else who was about to try his luck. The noise of the crowd seemed to reach him from a great distance. The next moment he was on top of the chute looking down at his own horse, Sleepy Sam!

A stubborn hope that Sleepy Sam might live up to his name vanished with that first glance of the beast. The brute lunged sideways, showing a wicked eye. Words that Orrin had overheard came back to him. "Just little old ponies that don't know much about bucking." In no time at all the handlers were helping him on Sleepy Sam.

Through Orrin's concentration blared the word from the loud-speakers, "Orrin Toler riding Sleepy Sam out of chute No. 3!" He gripped the surcingle, let his heels swing outward according to the rules, and saw the open space of the arena rushing to meet him.

Every sense was alert now. He tried to anticipate every move of the horse and to throw his own weight in the same direction while keeping his heels moving in a kicking motion.

After a quick bolt into the arena Sleepy Sam began to buck, twisting and landing stiff-legged. Orrin felt his body slide forward once, and in his imagination he had already been thrown, but he caught his balance and held on. As his black hair tossed this way and that, he wondered if he had equaled the time of the other riders. He was almost ready to welcome a trip to the dust in order to avoid the pounding that Sleepy Sam was giving him.

A series of little crow hops followed, which were much easier to judge. Why didn't the whistle blow? Orrin dared to hope that Sleepy Sam was tiring, when suddenly the horse reared so high it seemed he would fall over backward. Hastily Orrin drew his leg up along the horse's flank so that he could have a chance to jump clear. *Umff!* Sleepy Sam abruptly dropped back to four feet, bucking hard with head bent low.

All at once Orrin saw the exact spot on the ground where he was going to land. Even as he went he felt lucky, for he slid rather than flew from the horse. Now if he could only avoid the hoofs! There he lay in a heap on the ground like an experienced cowboy while the judges bore down on Sleepy Sam and led him away. He smothered his desire to get up and run.

"A very good ride!" The announcement reached Orrin as he got to his feet, dusty and smelling of horse dung. "Five and three-tenths seconds for Orrin Toler!"

As far as Orrin knew, his was the longest ride up to

that time, but there was no way of knowing how the judges were scoring the quality of each ride.

Five and three-tenths was still the best time when the final entrant on Warrior sprang from the chute. Orrin watched anxiously as this horse spun and bucked without appearing to disturb the rider at all. "I suppose I shouldn't want him to be thrown," Orrin muttered, "but it's the only way I can win the money."

The seconds, which had gone so slowly when Orrin was riding, seemed to race now. Either Warrior was not in the same class as the other horses, or else his rider's experience made it look easy.

Orrin's shoulders began to sag. Suddenly he felt the wilting intensity of the sun. He started to edge along the chutes toward the gate, when a quick groan rose from the audience. The sound pulled his gaze back to the arena where Warrior, freed of his rider, plunged in a haze of gray dust.

"Another excellent ride!" cried the announcer. "Ladies and Gentlemen, Elbridge Mace's ride lasted seven and one-tenth seconds. This concludes the bareback riding for novices."

There was a pause while the judges checked their scores, and then came the announcement: "The winner of the prize money—Elbridge Mace!"

Orrin leaned weakly against the nearest rail and ran a dirty hand across his perspiring forehead. "There goes three *hundred* smackers—besides my entry fee."

The woman who had taken Orrin's name for the event called to him with a gay smile as he passed, "Nice riding, *Amigo*. Better luck next time!"

"Thanks," Orrin said, stepping faster, as if he had brushed against a cactus.

Directly in front of him was an exit gate, promising relief from the uproar and color and the screaming brass. But through all the racket he could hear a girl's penetrating voice, "Orrin! Hey, Orrin!"

A figure ran awkwardly toward him, pausing on one foot to apologize for bumping a stranger's arm. Orrin saw a pair of intent brown eyes, a pair of braids swinging against a plaid shirt, and groaned, "That does it . . . Barbara Johnson saw me ride!"

But Barbara's big eyes were frankly admiring. She stood beside him, arms bent self-consciously, one hand resting on her hip. "You were really—*good!*" she exclaimed.

"Surprised you, eh?" Orrin retorted.

"I just wanted to tell you," she said with a queer, serious twist to her mouth. "You were better than El-bridge Mace. His horse wasn't so ornery as yours."

"Well—thanks," Orrin answered, with less bitterness.

"I—I wanted to tell you . . . " Barbara went on, but the rest of her words were lost. She looked around several times, then turned suddenly. "I'm home from school now. Well—so long," and she started away.

For a brief space Orrin's expression cleared. "I suppose she was trying to be nice," he reflected. Then he thought of losing the prize money, added it to his failure to make Old Man Caldwell pay the vet's bill, and muttered despondently, "I'm not doing any good for anybody."

11. Two Busy Years

THE sun had crossed the blue span overhead and hung in the west ready to begin its long slide downward when Orrin returned to Sunset Hill Ranch. Disappointment shadowed his deep-set eyes and held his mouth to an unvarying line. His hopes of handing over prize money to Clara Martin had penetrated deeper than he had realized.

The young palomino was eagerly pushing her soft muzzle across the top rail of the inclosure when Orrin approached. A bit of straw that she had been poking at clung rakishly to the side of her mouth; she cocked her head and nickered. Orrin whistled and the filly made a pleased, throaty sound in reply.

The soothing effect of Cloud's companionship had

barely brought back Orrin's grin when he saw Mrs. Martin crossing the barnyard.

"You were gone so long I was 'most ready to phone the police," she said lightly, but with relief in her smile. "Seems like worrying comes easy since Blacky was hurt. Good thing you're the steady kind."

Orrin was embarrassed. He was not ready to talk about the rodeo, so he ruffled Cloud's mane and said nothing.

Mrs. Martin went on, "Of course, you couldn't have spent the afternoon in a safer place than in the library."

Orrin struggled against an obstinate desire to remain silent. He wanted to stare into Cloud's shiny coat and forget his failures.

"I reckon you want to make up for lost time with Cloud," Mrs. Martin said, and started to leave.

Orrin blurted, "I didn't go to the library. I mean—I did go—but then I went to the rodeo."

"Why shouldn't you?" Mrs. Martin said. "You're man enough to come and go as you please."

"I mean, well—I entered the novices' bronc riding."

Clara Martin's eyelids dropped a little and a worn look appeared on her face. "We shouldn't expect you to give up the things you want to do."

"It was only so I could help out with some extra money." Orrin felt he was talking like a yokel.

But Mrs. Martin looked up quickly, her eyes were warm and shining. "It wasn't worth the risk, but I reckon I'm proud of you for trying."

Golden Cloud suddenly tossed her head and scampered off through the pasture gate. The sunlight formed shimmering pools of molten gold that flowed across her back and barrel.

Orrin asked hesitantly, "How about Buck? Will Blacky have to sell him?"

"We'll sit tight for the present." Mrs. Martin carefully

considered her words. "We'll try to hold what we have, except for the red calf. That's being sold."

Orrin noticed the length of Cloud's shadow as she stopped to nose at a twisted piece of baling wire near the gate so he knew it was time to milk. He said to Mrs. Martin, "Let's milk the cows. I'll go chase them in from pasture."

As early summer passed, Orrin felt a deepening sense of permanence at Sunset Hill. Blacky's broken bones had mended nicely, and he was doing a full day's work again. The rancher seemed more serious about his property now, and Clara's careworn look was beginning to disappear. Orrin could see the change take place in her, and he was really glad.

With Blacky's recovery, Orrin lost the impelling drive to rebuild the ranch single-handed, but he still had a quick eye to discover work that needed to be done and the energy to do it. One day as he was patching the barn roof, Tad Johnson rode in on his bay. Tad called his customary "Hey!" and watched Orrin nail down a sheet of aluminum, while the horse reached for the strip of grass outside the paddock fence.

"Hello there." Orrin put down the hammer and rested his hand, as he shook the perspiration from his forehead. "Where you going?"

"Riding down to the branch with Barbara. She's been listening to some talk about wild horses watering there. Come on along."

Orrin shook his head. "Too busy."

"Barbara's cutting across yonder by the corn. She'd like you to go, but she's too shy to ask."

"*She* wants me to go?"

"Sure does," Tad grinned knowingly. "She says you're

the only boy she ever liked. I reckon you made a hit with her that day at the rodeo."

Orrin had a queer feeling of being pleased, but he frowned at Tad. "Tell her I don't have time."

Tad pulled on the reins. "Get your head up out of that grass," he commanded the bay, and jogged off with a jaunty, "See you, Orrin."

Orrin reached for the hammer again and gave it an impatient shake. What was the matter with him? Was he really sorry he hadn't gone riding with Barbara? The question was hardly worth trying to answer.

He thought little more about the girl until they met at the Martin's mailbox the following week. As he looked down the road, he had seen her riding toward him. There was no mistaking the girl's easy grace, the rhythmic blending of motion of horse and rider. But as she came closer, the boy could see a frown on her tanned face.

At his cheerful hello she reluctantly reined in her horse. Orrin patted Spice's trim-muscled shoulder. "You don't seem very glad to see me," he ventured.

"Of course I am," she said distantly. "But naturally, if you couldn't find time to go riding yesterday. . . ."

"I had more important things to do."

"Thanks," Barbara replied tartly. Her cheeks turned the color of weathered tile. "Get along, Spice."

The horse wheeled so quickly that Orrin had to step backward to avoid being brushed.

Afraid that he had hurt her feelings, Orrin asked with a friendly smile, "Did you see any wild horses the other day?" but Spice's quick hoofs were already biting into the shoulder of the road, and Barbara did not look back.

"If she likes me so much as Tad says," Orrin muttered to himself, "she has an awful funny way of showing it." Then after a doubtful reflection he thought, "I suppose it wasn't very flattering to tell her I had more important things to do than to go riding with her."

Orrin did not see Barbara again to talk to during her summer vacation. When he went riding, it was usually within the boundaries of Sunset Hill Ranch. Sometimes he would ride to a high point and gaze off to the west across empty lands, and he would feel vaguely restless and lonely. But a pounding gallop back to the barn, followed by a session with Cloud in the little training corral, would soon shake off the mood.

The year passed swiftly at Sunset Hill. The cattle had freshened with no loss to cows or calves, and once more Mrs. Martin was talking of buying a pedigreed bull.

Golden Cloud was a magnificent yearling by this time, her lustrous coat indicating perfect condition. Her mane, which had lost its scrubbiness, spilled over her neck in a spray of silver. Her tail, high-arched, shone like a matching plume.

Since early spring Blacky himself had directed her training, guiding Orrin through the maze of steps necessary to produce a finished hunter. First, Cloud had been trained to bit and surcingle. Then she had learned to respond to long reins held by Orrin as he walked behind her. Following several weeks of this hand driving, Blacky had introduced a breaking harness so that the filly could be hitched to a breaking cart and driven for short turns. Finally, with full saddle and stirrups, she had been guided at the end of a lunge line, until she became accustomed to the stirrups flapping against her sides.

As Orrin pulled the girth tight under Cloud's belly, Blacky said, "Take her into the stall, Orrin. She's ready now to feel somebody in the saddle."

While Orrin stood at Cloud's head, Blacky swung into

the saddle. A quiver ran through Golden Cloud's body and her ears flattened, but Orrin talked gently to her and held her head. In a moment her muscles began to loosen and her ears pricked forward in normal curiosity.

"There now, easy," Blacky soothed her as he sat quietly on her back. After a short time he dismounted, and praised Cloud for her behavior by stroking her forehead and patting her shoulder.

"Could I— would it be all right for me to mount her now?" Orrin asked.

"Not yet," Blacky advised, "I'm a mite heavy for her myself, and I'm lighter than you are."

Blacky mounted and dismounted several more times until he turned to Orrin with a pleased shake of his head. "She's coming along fine. I never worked with a likelier filly."

After the formal lesson there always followed a brief period practicing tricks in the training corral. It was then that the palomino showed where her interest really lay; for, although she was learning obediently under lunge line and saddle, she fairly nickered her delight every time Orrin took her through the gate across the paddock.

When Blacky had unsaddled Cloud, Orrin threw open the back door of the stall and walked out without a backward glance, snapping his fingers softly at his side as a signal. When he passed through the paddock into the training corral, he felt a gentle push against his back, and there was Cloud, warm gold and silver, right behind him.

Orrin gave signals for every trick, but it was part of the game for Cloud to guess his wishes through his words and actions without the use of any aid. Orrin carelessly dropped his handkerchief on the ground, walked to the fence and stood with his back to the horse.

In a moment there was a nudging against the boy's

hand, and Orrin's fingers picked the handkerchief from Cloud's lips. "Nice going," Orrin grinned, rewarding Cloud with a piece of bread.

One after another Cloud performed her tricks. Sometimes she needed a repetition of the signal, more often she cannily guessed Orrin's meaning, so that the boy himself hardly knew how she had sensed it. She knelt, she bowed, she lay on her side, she rolled on her back and pawed the air—tricks they had picked up one at a time. Throughout the practice Cloud showed a patience that was amazing at her age. But when Orrin finally turned her into the pasture, she immediately proved that she was still a strong, frisky yearling as she galloped along the fence.

By the time winter weather interrupted Cloud's training as a hunter, she had learned to carry a rider around the training corral at a walk. During the fall Orrin and Blacky had built a small jumping course with jumps about a foot high. The filly had taken easily to jumping over the obstacles while Orrin or Blacky guided her from the end of a lunge rope.

Although this work had stopped for the time being, Orrin continued to school Cloud in the tricks she knew, refining them and adding several new ones. Blacky often lost patience and said to the boy, "When are you going to stop wasting your time on that nonsense?"

And Orrin often replied just as stubbornly, "My time isn't being wasted." Then Blacky would grunt and forget about it for a while.

When at last the early Oklahoma spring brought an end to the winter rain and snow, Blacky had Orrin start lunging Cloud to get her in condition for more advanced training.

As she progressed into her two-year-old summer, Cloud learned to trot and canter, while Orrin rode. The filly was nearly full-grown now and stunningly beautiful. When she stood flank to flank with Queen, the two satiny heads were almost even, although Queen was still the heavier of the two.

One hot day in the summer Orrin was in the training corral teaching Cloud to dance. Barbara and Tad Johnson sat on the fence watching. It was the first time he had seen Barbara since the previous summer, and he had been surprised how much she had changed. She was more grown up and poised, and when she dismounted she walked without stumbling. She greeted Orrin by saying that she had not see him at the Frontier Club, but somehow he hadn't minded, and when he invited her to stay to watch Golden Cloud's training he was glad she accepted.

As he glanced up, he saw Barbara looking at Cloud with a breathless, admiring expression and a glow in her eyes that gave her face an entirely new appearance. Why, the girl really wasn't bad-looking, was she?

"Watch Cloud now," Orrin boasted. "She's picked most of this up herself." He cupped a harmonica in his hands, slid it across his lips and began to play the "Blue Danube Waltz."

Gracefully Cloud lifted her forefeet high, giving a quaint little hop at intervals and swaying slightly all the time. Orrin played faster and Cloud's steps came more quickly and less mincing. She tossed her head from side to side, making her mane ripple in the sunshine. At the end of the piece she bowed her head. Barbara clapped her hands while Tad whistled.

"Do it again!" Barbara cried as Orrin held out a piece of carrot to Golden Cloud.

"Wait a minute. I want to show you something else." Orrin's face was flushed with pleasure. It was the first time Cloud had performed for any outsiders, and he sensed the filly's power over the boy and girl. If Cloud could please them, she could influence any audience. He had been right when he had told Blacky that teaching her tricks was not a waste of time.

"I've been teaching her to pose," Orrin went on. "See what you think of this." He patted Cloud's neck, meanwhile talking quietly to her. Then he began to fix her in position. Her forelegs he placed straight and even, hind legs slightly back of normal, head tilted up and to one side, tail lifted high. He ruffled her mane with a sweep of his hand and then he stood back. "I'll soon have her doing it by herself," he told Barbara and Tad.

There was a wild, beautiful look about the palomino as she stood there motionless, a mingling of all the fire and freedom of her ancestry, and Barbara and Tad were so entranced that they did not even glance at Orrin.

"Orrin, are you there?" It was Mrs. Martin's voice from the barnyard.

That put an end to the pose. Cloud turned her head at the voice, stamped a hind foot, and swished her tail in quite an ordinary manner.

"Coming," Orrin called back to Mrs. Martin.

Tad slid down from the fence and gave an expressive whistle. "You've sure got something there, Orrin. Come on, Barbara. Let's get going."

But Barbara continued to stand in front of Cloud, stroking the soft head and talking in a low, coaxing voice. The filly pointed her ears forward and gave a contented whinny, but her eyes were turned to Orrin.

"Come on," Tad cried impatiently. "That's not your horse."

"I know. But she likes me. Don't you, Cloud?" Barbara looked earnestly at Orrin. "Is it O.K. if I come and see her again?"

"Sure," Orrin replied, "any time." He threw open the

corral gate, laughed as Cloud romped out into the paddock, and went to meet Mrs. Martin.

"There's something you should know about," Clara said.

Orrin asked quickly, "What is it?"

"Gabe is coming here again."

Orrin replied heavily, "When?"

"Soon. He mailed a letter from Waco the day before yesterday. Orrin, he's asking for the east room, and he wanted to know how his palomino is doing."

"He has no right to!" Orrin cried angrily, looking out into the paddock. The muscles around his mouth twitched. "Gabe better stay away from Cloud."

Clara's eyes looked troubled, but her voice was steady. "Let's not be hasty, Orrin. We can't run away from a promise made in good faith."

"He'll never have Cloud!" The words burst through the tightness in Orrin's throat.

"You've raised her and trained her. It's natural you should feel that way, she being such a pretty thing, too. I know, because I've grown right fond of my heifers, plain and slow-witted as they are."

"Why don't we tell him to go somewhere else? Mrs. Martin, do we have to jump every time he opens his mouth?"

Mrs. Martin's eyes flashed, then the flare died away. "It wouldn't be the honorable thing to do," she replied calmly.

As Orrin left the paddock, his legs moved slowly. He reached for the iron latch on the stable door with a labored movement. Up to this point, he had avoided thinking about Gabe; he had not permitted himself to accept the reality of Gabe's claim to Golden Cloud.

Golden Cloud's saddle sprawled inside on the stable floor; Orrin gathered it in his arms and carried it to the

tack room. He hung it on a wooden peg next to a heavy
stock saddle and glanced about the well-ordered room.
Every bit of leather hung in place, suppled with neat's-
foot oil that he had rubbed in with his own fingers. The
pegs that held the bridles still showed the clean strokes
of an ax. He had cut them himself from a seasoned plank.
. . All for Gabe to use!

The tang of leather, which usually gave Orrin a brisk
feeling, now smelled mildly nauseating. He pushed open
the door to the paddock with his foot, hesitated in the
doorway, and whistled to Cloud.

She tossed up her head, pointed her ears at Orrin and
raced headlong for him. Her tail plumed out in the
wind and the thick hair in her mane lifted and flickered
like irregular prongs of white flame.

A cool, drawling voice cut in behind Orrin. "Still playing with Tubby, eh?"

Orrin felt the muscles across his chest and at the base
of his neck contract. He took several quick breaths,
steadied himself, and turned around slowly just as Cloud
arrived with a rush and ruffle of hoofbeats. Her muzzle
pushed the back of Orrin's shoulder as he faced Gabe
Martin.

Gabe was squinting through the rolling ball of dust
kicked up by the hoofs, looking past Orrin and measuring the filly with admiration in his eyes. He made a
whistling sound through his lips and held out his hand,
rubbing his finger tips together.

Cloud stretched her nose past Orrin and took a step
forward.

"Back," Orrin ordered Cloud sharply, but he was
watching Gabe. Warily Orrin slid his feet apart in a
wrestler's broad stance and bent forward slightly at the
waist. His actions were as clear as if he had drawn a
line on the ground and warned Gabe not to cross it.

Although the dust had billowed past, Gabe's eyes were still half shut; but the narrowed lids did not conceal their intent. He ignored Orrin and spoke to Cloud. "Wait till I throw a saddle on you and show everybody how we ride in Texas."

Cloud stamped impatiently and rubbed against Orrin, unmindful of the anger that was rising in her master.

Gabe stepped back a pace, showing by his deliberate movements that he was not retreating, but going of his own accord. "I'll see you," he told Cloud, and then added, "after we make a few changes around here."

Like a sentry, Orrin waited at the paddock, and the longer he stayed the darker his thoughts became. Why hadn't he admitted to himself right along that this was Gabe's home and that Cloud was only being raised here? Three years had seemed like such an endless time when Blacky and Gabe had made their agreement, and now Orrin realized with a pang that there was only one year left. If he had stumbled face to face with a cougar while out hunting doves, he would not have been brought to realization any harder.

At other times when Orrin's world had become a black wall pressing against him, he had gone to Cloud. But suddenly the filly's power to reassure him had weakened. She had become transparent, a thing without permanence. Orrin felt an overwhelming need to find Clara Martin and talk to her.

Orrin was pretty sure that Mrs. Martin was in the house, but he knew that Gabe was there too and so he decided to try the dairy first. He started off the short way, over the fence and up the bank.

A door closed at the ranch house, loud enough for Orrin to hear. He stopped on the uphill side of the driveway and looked back. There were voices, and then Orrin could see Gabe striding down to the stable. It was as plain as if Gabe had shouted that he was going for a ride.

Orrin stepped behind a mulberry tree and watched Gabe through its branches. The boy stood motionless while Gabe went into the barn for a saddle. His fists closed until the skin stretched white over the knuckles. If Gabe tried to throw a saddle on Cloud, he'd be sorry!

A distraction came from the direction of the house as somebody gunned the pickup's motor, but Orrin's eyes did not turn from the pasture where Cloud, Queen, Ripple and Buck were cropping grass. Then the tack-room door banged and Gabe appeared, carrying saddle and bridle.

Orrin bent down for a clearer view. His knees began to tremble like a sprinter's before a race. Through an angry haze he watched Gabe balance the saddle on the pasture fence and whistle to Cloud.

A tense moment followed, and then Orrin saw that Gabe had only been teasing Cloud. He really wanted Ripple. However, Orrin did not breathe regularly again until Ripple was saddled and Gabe had ridden her out of sight in his scatter-dash style.

Orrin remembered that he had started out to find Mrs. Martin, and without bothering with the dairy now, he went directly to the house.

Mrs. Martin gave Orrin a welcoming smile, and they talked about the hot weather and patching the barn roof. There was something about being near her that made Orrin feel new confidence. But twice he hesitated before he asked, "Is Gabe going to stay long?"

Mrs. Martin dropped some darning into her lap and looked silently out of the living-room window. The soft curve of her cheek seemed to grow taut. "Blacky told him to make himself at home." She was still partly turned away from Orrin.

"What did Gabe say?"

"When he saw that Blacky hadn't changed any, he cut loose with a lot of fine talk about himself."

"Does he—still have the chestnut filly?"

"He claims he has her," Mrs. Martin answered quietly. "He bragged about how gentle she is."

Strength flowed from Orrin's arms and shoulders. He had to go somewhere; he did not want Mrs. Martin to look into his face, so he dragged out the back door.

As he left, he barely heard her say, "Gabe's smug talk riled Blacky so much that he sold out of here in the pickup faster than I ever saw him travel."

Orrin walked on past the paddock and pasture without even stopping to respond to Golden Cloud's nicker. His cheeks burned as much from the trouble inside the house as from the hot sun and wind outside. He had to get used to the idea of seeing Cloud go. After next year he knew that Gabe would not return to Sunset Hill. Then Orrin would devote all his time to improving the ranch. He would be Mrs. Martin's faithful partner.

Orrin was hardly aware of direction as he left the drive and pushed through weeds and brush. He stopped on a hilltop and stared into space, then down that hill and up another. The breeze dried the perspiration from his skin before it had a chance to form into drops. He stopped again and was about to continue when he saw motion below.

A rider was charging recklessly at top speed across the gullied valley. It was dangerous going. Orrin felt sorry for the horse, who was risking a broken leg at every stride. It was then that he saw it was Ripple.

Before Orrin could shout to Gabe to slow down, Ripple stumbled and fell, throwing her rider in front of her. In an instant Gabe was on his feet, slashing at Ripple with a quirt while she struggled to a sitting position.

"Stop that!" Orrin yelled as he went crashing down the hill toward Gabe.

Twice Gabe's quirt rose and licked out before he saw Orrin. His whip arm was drawing up for a third fling when Orrin cried angrily, "Gabe! Gabe!"

As Gabe whirled, he took a step toward Orrin and his quirt jerked back higher over his shoulder.

Orrin involuntarily squinted his eyes and threw up his arm to protect his face, but he did not stop advancing.

"It's you," Gabe growled, letting his quirt drop slowly to his side. His eyes blazed with fury, but he was making an effort to control himself.

Ripple had lurched to her feet, and with empty stirrups banging against her sides, was jogging ahead to safety. Orrin whistled to her and she stopped doubtfully, but made no effort to return.

Gabe's voice was thick. "You were spying on me."

"No! I saw you running Ripple too hard and wanted to slow you down."

Gabe's chest swelled indignantly and Orrin kept his eyes on the quirt, noticing at the same time that Gabe did not look so big as he had at one time. Two years of ranch life had added to Orrin's height and had given him almost as much muscle as Gabe.

Muttering, Gabe coiled up the quirt and stuffed it into his hip pocket. "Trying to make a good boy of me, eh? You want to be sure I get the palomino fair and square."

Orrin said nothing in reply to this. If he had not interfered, Gabe would have cut Ripple up so badly that Blacky might have disposed of Gabe's claim to Cloud at once, regardless of how the chestnut filly was being handled.

A crafty look came into Gabe's face. "When I put Ripple back into pasture, nobody will know anything

154

happened—including you if you're smart. Blacky never did like a squealer."

Orrin watched gloomily while Gabe, with guileful patience, started after Ripple. He could see that it would be only a matter of time before the horse was caught.

The afternoon was passing, but the thought of going to work was distasteful to Orrin. He now wandered aimlessly back toward the ranch, stopping once for a considerable time to watch a red ant force his way through a tangle of weeds with a dead cricket.

At intervals Orrin drew long, slow breaths. Nothing seemed to matter much. There was no satisfaction in wishing that he had not seen Gabe. Poor Ripple had taken enough punishment as it was, but stopping Gabe had been practically the same as giving Cloud away. It was rough, but what could he do?

Eventually Orrin found himself on the driveway near the ranch house. He knew that he was late for milking. Nothing was right this afternoon.

Mrs. Martin must have seen him, for she was coming to meet him. Orrin had a guilty feeling that she had been looking for him.

"He's gone," Mrs. Martin said, hardly glancing at Orrin. "I don't know what Blacky will say."

"Gabe's gone?" Orrin stammered.

"He rode in as nice as you please, gave Ripple a good sponging and rubdown and turned her into pasture. But when he talked to me the very devil was in him. He stormed around because the east room wasn't ready, and I couldn't stand it. I told him he could have the spare room or nothing . . . Well, he's gone. He said if that was the way we kept our promises, he wouldn't stay."

Orrin frowned; he could see how it was. Gabe had managed things so that Blacky would feel under increased obligation to him. For a moment Orrin decided to tell Clara what had just happened, then he changed his mind. It wouldn't help to tattletale. Clara would believe him, but Blacky would never listen to him. The rancher was stubborn, and prided himself too much on his justness to be influenced by a story that could not be proved. Orrin's information would only make him favor Gabe more.

The boy looked moodily at Clara. "I guess I'll get on with the chores."

12. The Deal with the Carnival

BY SUPPERTIME, when Blacky returned to the ranch, his wife seemed perfectly composed. If she was disturbed about the way he would take the news of Gabe's leaving, she did not show it. Her voice was pleasant but firm, and she showed due consideration for Blacky's principles. But she made it clear that the incident was over now and closed. Gabe had made the decision himself; he had not been turned away.

Orrin watched Blacky's face take on a stubborn cast, but when the ranchman spoke, his tone was surprisingly mild. "If he comes back, let me talk to him, hear?"

"I sure will," Clara answered, as she handed Orrin a handful of silverware to put on the table.

There was nothing more said about Gabe during the meal or afterwards or even in the days that followed.

But in many subtle ways, when Clara was talking to Orrin alone, she managed to inject some common-sense ideas that gradually became part of Orrin's thinking. Disappointments had to be expected she said. That was the way of life. It was a sign that one was maturing when one could take these without bitterness. Orrin even found that he could go on training Cloud, although for a while it seemed completely without purpose.

Surprisingly enough, it was Blacky who changed this. Since he had given up visiting the Frontier Club, there had been no occasions when he and Orrin had been drawn together in a spirit of good fellowship. Orrin sometimes had the feeling that Blacky was becoming more and more critical of him.

Blacky had made a hurried trip to Oklahoma City for some iron pipe so he could replace a few lengths that had rusted out in the water line to the dairy barn. Orrin was bracing the good pipe with a Stillson wrench while Blacky undid the coupling that held the rusted section. Their heads were bent down; neither was talking. With a final grunt, Blacky forced the coupling loose and straightened up to clear the perspiration from his eyes and to catch his breath.

"Saw Luke Campbell in the city today," Blacky said gruffly.

That name meant nothing to Orrin.

"He's a small-time show man; just sort of pops up now and then. He wants a headline act for a carnival next spring, and I told him about Cloud."

"A trick act?" Orrin was not sure he had understood Blacky.

"I reckon she can do it. Luke's going to drop by and give her the once-over."

Excitement began to penetrate Orrin's thinking. Finally he cried, "I hope I can get in some more practice before he shows up."

That afternoon, when Orrin met Cloud at the pasture gate, there was an eagerness in his voice that had been missing for days. "We've got to get to work in a hurry," he said to her briskly, and Cloud whinnied contentedly as if she knew what he meant.

Each day after that Orrin spent almost as much time with currycomb and rub rag as he did in the training corral. Never had Cloud's coat had such a rich sheen, never had it been so responsive to changing lights and shadows.

The day Luke Campbell came, Cloud was grazing in the pasture, and Orrin was afraid she wouldn't be looking her best.

Campbell was a heavy man, with small, sleepy-looking eyes. He was wearing a natty two-toned brown shirt with fancy stitching. Orrin took the business card that Luke offered him and acknowledged Blacky's introduction by shaking hands.

"Well, where is she?" Campbell asked in a wheezy voice.

"Thisaway," Blacky replied.

They stopped on the driveway, where they could look across the paddock to the pasture. "There she is yonder," Blacky replied, pointing to the beautiful palomino.

With a deep wrinkling of his forehead Luke Campbell opened his eyes wider. "Hm-m," he grunted after a long look.

"She could stand a grooming," Orrin said anxiously.

"I reckon so," Campbell replied dryly.

They stopped again at the pasture gate and Orrin whistled. Up came Cloud's head, and with mane and tail flying, she galloped over to him.

The furrows in Mr. Campbell's forehead deepened

until his eyes were nearly round. "She's right pretty," he admitted.

Campbell and Blacky stayed in the paddock and looked over the fence while Orrin and Cloud went into the corral.

"There, girl. There, girl," Orrin soothed Cloud as he patted her neck, but he was really more nervous than the filly.

From the very beginning, when Orrin had started training Cloud, he had talked about paid performances, but he never had thought out clearly just who would hire them. That phase of his idea had been screened by the same indistinct haze that dims faraway landmarks, although the immediate trail may be plain enough. Now here was actually a promoter standing by ready to talk business if he liked what he saw. Orrin could think of a dozen reasons why Luke Campbell would not be satisfied.

Orrin held Cloud by her white forelock and led her around gently until her glossy flank was turned to the two men. He stepped away and found a lilac switch that he had left in a corner of the corral.

"Bow," said Orrin, making a slight motion with the switch.

Golden Cloud bent back a slim foreleg, at the same time dipping her head and swinging it toward the audience.

"Lie down," Orrin commanded.

The filly obeyed, with no other aid than the sound of Orrin's voice.

Orrin gave his switch a quick turn. "Roll over."

The palomino gave her head a toss, threw up her hoofs, and over she went. Another signal from Orrin, and she rolled back again. When she stood up, she was covered with dust and bits of grass. Orrin tried to brush her coat with his hand. He should not have asked her to do this trick; or at least he should have saved it for the end.

Luke Campbell seemed amused by Cloud's appearance. He chuckled as he looked at his watch. "I reckon you've shown me enough."

"I wanted you to see some of her poses," Orrin exclaimed.

"They'll wait," Luke Campbell wheezed. "You work all her tricks into one good act and she'll be ready."

"You mean—for the carnival?" Orrin asked.

Campbell looked at Blacky between half-closed lids. "She's your filly, Blacky. What do you reckon her act will be worth?"

Blacky answered cagily, "Time enough to settle that next spring."

"Figure you'll have me in a corner then, eh? Well, if your price gets too high, maybe I won't take her."

Blacky shrugged, and it was hard to tell whether or not he was acting. "If you don't want her, somebody else will. She'll draw a smart of customers."

Orrin fidgeted, hoping the men would come to a definite agreement, but they didn't. They seemed to enjoy the bargaining too much to close the deal.

Blacky and Luke parted after a few more good-natured thrusts. The promoter pressed Orrin's arm before leaving. "We'll be opening around the middle of May." He sank his hands in his hip pockets and studied Golden Cloud while he puckered his forehead. Then he gave his head a slow shake, as if finding the palomino something to wonder at.

"Next May," he said more briskly and walked to his car.

Orrin grinned at Cloud as he flicked the dead grass from her mane.

"We've got a job on our hands, kid."

He couldn't wait to see Mrs. Martin; and when he did tell her about Luke Campbell's visit, her enthusiasm amazed him.

She looked at his erect head and shoulders and laughed, "Now I know I'm going to buy that new dress. We're going to celebrate as soon as the carnival ends."

"Wait a minute," Orrin protested. "This isn't going to make us rich."

"I know," Clara answered quickly, "but we need a good excuse. Don't try to talk me out of it."

Orrin grinned, but he did not like to see her getting her hopes up so high. After all, everything between Blacky and Luke had been left undecided until the next spring.

Within another week Orrin's mood had adjusted to the circumstances as they existed now. He was no longer excited over the carnival nor depressed over Gabe's visit. His state of mind had acquired an evenness now that was almost like living in an unreal world. He realized that his answers came more slowly when he was spoken to; his actions were made more deliberately.

It wasn't that he had lost interest in Cloud's performing at the carnival. That was still tremendously important. His hours spent with her were really worth-while from a business standpoint. Most likely there would still be time after the carnival for several engagements with local rodeos. The money would go to the Martins and he would feel repaid for training Cloud. When Gabe came to claim her, Orrin would not have to feel that his time had been thrown away.

The days passed quickly, like the blades of a windmill rising, flashing, and tumbling after each other. By fall Blacky had eased off in working with Cloud. As he said, "She's jumping big, Orrin. She takes to it naturally. We won't push her."

Orrin knew this was so. He rode Cloud as often as he could, sometimes taking her over jumps, sometimes riding cross-country. He knew the surge of her body as she soared over the hurdles, the growing power in her stride. "She needs exercise," he would tell himself. "She's beginning to feel her oats."

September was a bad month that year in Oklahoma. Flash floods washed out roads and damaged winter wheat fields. A tornado had crossed the state border near Sallisaw and had ripped through several villages. This storm was too far away to endanger Sunset Hill Ranch, but the continued heavy rains ruined Blacky's first planting of wheat and he had to replant every acre.

After the autumn storms had ended, the weather had turned very dry and continued dry for month after month. Occasionally Clara would look hopefully overhead and say to Orrin, "We're going to have rain presently." But although the weather sometimes looked threatening, the usual heavy rains did not come.

The winter that followed was marked by careful economy at the ranch. Two of the three cows that freshened in December bore bull calves. These were sold for veal, but being of the lightweight Jersey strain, their value was small.

Through it all Orrin stuck to the task of perfecting Cloud's routine. He had arranged the tricks carefully so that the act began with the handkerchief trick, progressed through more difficult ones until the horse did her dance to his harmonica music. As the climax, he used the pose that Barbara Johnson had liked so much. He thought to himself that he would call this pose "The Spirit of the Great Southwest."

In March, Queen was to drop another foal. Blacky was just as concerned about the mare now as he had been of her before Cloud's birth, and he hoped just as hard that this foal would be a palomino also. Orrin tried his best to keep this event foremost in his mind. He slept in the barn the last few nights and watched over Queen attentively.

When the foal was born, Queen looked proudly at the wobbly sorrel colt that nuzzled against her, but Blacky was badly disappointed. Orrin waited his chance to wander outside where he could watch Cloud searching for the scarce patches of new grass.

That same day Tad Johnson stopped to see the new foal. "I've got to report to Barbara," he grinned. "Boy, she'll be mad when she hears it's only a little old sorrel."

"I suppose she'll be coming home before long," Orrin remarked absently.

"Next week," Tad replied. "It's spring vacation."

"Well, tell her to ride over and take a look at the colt if she wants to." Orrin noticed how easily Tad could throw himself up on his horse's bare back; the youngster's legs were certainly growing long.

It hardly seemed more than a day or two later that Orrin looked out the living-room window and saw a girl riding up the drive. He had finished lunch and was glancing at an old copy of *Capper's Farmer*, but when he recognized Barbara he dropped the magazine and hurried outside.

"Hey!" Barbara called.

Her voice sounded more pleasing, somewhat fuller than Orrin had remembered. "Hello, Barbara," he called. "I guess you heard about the colt's being a sorrel."

"Too bad," Barbara smiled as she bent down to slap at a fly on Spice's shoulder, "but I bet he's cute anyway."

"Come on, get down," Orrin said, "and I'll show him to you."

Barbara dismounted and tied Spice's reins to the barnyard fence. "The ranch looks a lot better since you've been working here," she remarked.

The way she said it made Orrin feel glad he had taken so much interest in the place. "There's lots more to do," he said, "but it takes time."

"You sure deserve a lot of credit."

"Thanks." As they walked to the stable, Orrin told her about his ideas for terracing the west fields and putting them to use. Barbara listened so attentively that Orrin talked steadily until they stood at Queen's stall.

"Oh, he *is* cute!" Barbara cried when she spied the colt. "There's nothing so pretty as a baby colt or filly. And isn't Queen the proud mama."

Orrin smiled along with the girl as she exclaimed about the colt's long ears and startled expression.

"Now I want to see Golden Cloud," she said, and Orrin felt pleased that he could do something more for her.

"She's in the pasture," Orrin replied. "We'll go out through the tack room."

When they spied Cloud grazing on the pasture slope, Barbara asked, "Does she still come running when you whistle?"

Orrin did not feel so talkative now. "She'll come," he said soberly and gave one short whistle. Cloud broke into a run, mane and tail streaming like spray blown back from the top of a breaker. She pointed her ears and turned her head as she ran, until she saw where Orrin was standing. Then over she raced in a sweeping, golden curve and stood blowing through her nostrils while Orrin reached over the fence to stroke her.

Barbara's eyes were warm and glowing. "Doesn't it do something to you when you see her tear around like that? So beautiful and free. Like watching an eagle swooping through the sky."

Orrin kept his gaze fixed on Cloud's shoulder and said nothing.

Barbara seemed to understand how he felt. She stood quietly until he turned to her. Then she asked, "How are the tricks coming?"

"Swell . . ." He hesitated, feeling a strong urge to talk again. He would tell her all about the carnival and let her watch Cloud's routine. Nobody but himself had seen the complete act. He had been planning to show it first to Mrs. Martin.

"Cloud is smarter than ever," Orrin added, but the impulse to say anything more had passed.

They walked slowly to the place where Spice was waiting. Barbara was talking about school and the rides she hoped to take during vacation. She changed the subject once to say with a puzzled smile, "I can't get over it, Orrin. You seem so much older—or is it my imagination?"

Orrin laughed briefly. "No, it's not your imagination. I'm nearly twenty."

Before she left, they had agreed to go riding together on Monday. Barbara was anxious to see how Cloud looked carrying a rider. As the girl rode off, Orrin stood on the back porch, where he could catch glimpses of her and Spice as they crossed the fields. Then he thought about Cloud and the carnival, and realizing that it was already Easter time, he muttered to himself, "I wonder why we haven't heard from Luke Campbell."

13. A Boy and a Horse

THERE wasn't a word from Luke Campbell until the middle of April. Then he called up Ike Johnson's from Oklahoma City and left a message for Blacky and Orrin. He had been at a resort in southern California managing some kind of amusement center and had to go right back. As soon as he wound up his business there, he reported, he would get busy with the carnival. But it might be June before he could make all the arrangements for the opening.

After Blacky repeated the message to Orrin, he muttered, "I wonder if he figures he can beat us down on the price by playing hard to get?"

"You notice he still wants Cloud's act," Orrin said. But a twisting stab of irritation burned inside him. Why hadn't Blacky closed the deal with Campbell when he had had the chance? Now the whole thing might fall through, and if it did, it would be too late to sign up with a rodeo.

In May they heard from Luke again. He was going to loaf for a week or so, he said, and then return to Oklahoma. As soon as he got there, he would drop around at the ranch.

"Is he really going to do anything about a carnival?" Orrin asked Blacky despondently.

"He says he is," Blacky replied brusquely.

Orrin recalled one time when he was a small boy and his Uncle Chauncey had promised to buy him a football. After his uncle told him that the order had been placed, Orrin waited and waited. It was to be the grandest present he had ever had. Each time he asked about it, his uncle explained with increasing vagueness that sporting goods were slow in delivery. Orrin had kept his hopes up for a long, long time, but the football never arrived.

As the month of May slipped away, Orrin became convinced that Gabe would reach Sunset Hill before Luke Campbell did. The sessions with Cloud continued in the corral, but they had become desultory. Cloud knew her act well; she had known it for several months. Clara Martin had watched the routine from beginning to end and had praised it highly.

No longer did the carnival exist in Orrin's mind as a definite event, although it still held a shadowy place somewhere in the background. If he gave up the idea completely, there would be no reason for keeping Cloud in training.

One Saturday in June, when everything at the ranch seemed exactly like the preceding day, Luke Campbell appeared. He did not have the exact date for the opening of the carnival, but he was lining up the concessions.

Orrin stood in the background while Blacky and Luke

dickered over terms. The boy thought his interest in the carnival had died, but the longer the bargaining continued, the faster his pulse beat.

At last Luke said, "Let's put it like this. We'll run the palomino's picture in all the advertising, including the posters. Then we'll charge two bits admission for her act and split the gate fifty-fifty."

"That gives you a right fancy profit," Blacky said.

"I have to stand the cost of promoting the show," Luke countered.

Blacky glanced at Orrin and back to Luke. "All right, you hoss thief. It's a trade," and shook hands solemnly with Luke to make the agreement official.

Now that their business was concluded, the two men relaxed, and Blacky began to chuckle at Luke's stories of his experiences in California.

Orrin listened with a smile until he stopped to realize that the summer would be well along before the carnival could possibly be held. Then his face grew taut, and he remembered that Mrs. Martin wanted him to scrub the calf pen. He had to interrupt the conversation to ask Luke Campbell, "Do you want to see Cloud go through her act?"

Luke, still grinning over a remark of Blacky's, wheezed, "I reckon not, son. Blacky says she's good, and that's all I need to know. One suggestion, though. Could you start the thing off by whistling to her and have her come galloping from somewhere out of sight?"

Orrin considered for a moment before he said gravely, "Sure."

"I'll send a photographer around presently to take some shots of the palomino," Luke said; then he and Blacky resumed their banter, as if neither had another thing to think about.

Each day during June and July framed a lasting picture

in Orrin's mind. The knowledge of Gabe's inevitable coming was a gray backdrop against which everything else was outlined all the more brightly. Standing out in sharp relief was Clara Martin's affection and understanding, which always seemed to steady him.

When he had the time, he would ride past Johnson's and ask Barbara to join him. She had a habit of riding along quietly on Spice, enjoying the contrast of fluffy clouds against a gaunt landscape or watching the curved high lights slide over Cloud's body. But all the while she had a ready smile that made her good company.

About two weeks after the posters announcing Luke Campbell's carnival had been tacked on trees and telephone poles Blacky received a letter from Gabe. The rancher read the letter and handed it to Clara without speaking. After she finished reading it, she folded it, put it back into the envelope, and slowly hung up the dustcloth she had been using.

Orrin felt an indistinct, humming sensation in his ears, but he waited with outward indifference and in silence.

Clara Martin looked at Orrin. "About the third of August, Orrin. He's bringing the chestnut filly here in a trailer."

Orrin nodded and all three stared in different directions. The carnival was scheduled to run from the tenth to the twentieth of August.

Blacky cleared his throat. "You're going right ahead with the carnival, son."

"All right."

On the second day of August, Clara Martin gave the spare bedroom a thorough cleaning. It was plain that she was preparing the room for Gabe and had no intention of asking Orrin to move.

That same afternoon a scribbled post card from Gabe said that he was being delayed in Texas for business reasons. Instead of being relieved, Mrs. Martin said to Orrin, "Queer that he's so full of business all of a sudden. I wonder what he's up to now."

Gabe's business evidently took considerable time, for he had not yet arrived by the morning of the tenth.

Orrin wanted to reach the carnival grounds early so that Cloud would have a chance to get used to the noise and become accustomed to the field where she was to perform. Blacky was to stay at the ranch, but Clara was going with Orrin.

About nine o'clock Orrin drove to Johnson's to borrow their horse trailer. Barbara watched him hook it to the pickup, her eyes sparkling with excitement. "What time is the first show?" she asked. "I don't want to be late."

But Orrin had begun to feel nervous. "Why don't you wait until tomorrow?" he suggested awkwardly. "Everything will just be getting started today."

Barbara looked disappointed, until she took another look at Orrin's face. Then she smiled. "Well—I see what you mean. But I'll stay for both shows tomorrow to make up for it."

On the way back to Sunset Hill with the trailer, Orrin's doubts began to increase. Suppose Cloud wouldn't come to him in a strange place when he whistled? The boy could see the faces of the people in the audience if the act flopped—youngsters laughing and jeering at him, indignant women storming across the field to accuse him of being a cheat. He suddenly became painfully aware that he would be in the carnival too. Then he began to wonder if he should have borrowed a fancy cowboy outfit to wear. But it was too late now to think up a lot of ideas.

When Orrin led Cloud into the pickup, he was dressed much the same as usual, except for his wide-brimmed felt hat and high-heeled boots. His shirt was a red plaid that was slightly faded from the sun, and his blue levis were a trifle too small. As soon as he stopped at the house for Mrs. Martin, he asked her uneasily, "Do you think I look all right?"

Clara Martin smiled. "Just the way you should look. Nobody will notice you once they catch sight of Cloud."

The pickup gained speed slowly with the weight of the trailer behind it. Orrin got the feel of it pretty soon. "I hope Mr. Campbell has the field fixed up for us," Orrin said after driving a mile or so. "Day before yesterday when I went over there, nothing was ready."

"It's natural you should think about such things now," Clara said. "Wait until your show is over, and you'll be laughing at yourself."

"Yeah—I guess so."

The pickup's engine missed several times and slowed a little, then smoothed out again. Mrs. Martin said, "I reckon the old truck is feeling its age. The mechanic at the garage told Blacky it shouldn't be used until he overhauled it, but it's good for a few more miles, I hope."

Orrin nodded. The Martins might have had a new one by now if this year had not been so dry. But feed prices had gone up, and they even had to buy hay. If Cloud's act was successful, the money earned would be a big help.

They rode past a broad stretch of level land, bumped over a bridge that crossed a dry stream bed. The combination of blazing sun and overworked motor made the pickup cab uncomfortably warm.

"It's going to be hotter than yesterday," Orrin said. "I hope Cloud isn't minding the ride." He glanced out the open window. Dust hung suspended in the air at all times; and whenever the breeze blew, tawny columns of it sprang up from the fields, eddying and swirling into thin, brown clouds.

Orrin slowed down when he saw the bleak framework

of an oil derrick rising from the field at his left. In the distance, looking far out across the countryside, were the tops of the tall buildings of Oklahoma City. "We're almost there," he told Mrs. Martin.

A little farther on they came to the entrance of the carnival grounds, marked by flapping pennants strung on long ropes. Behind these were two rows of booths and amusements, and off at the sides a ferris wheel and carrousel. Orrin sat up straighter. "It looks a lot better today," he commented as he drove into the parking area. "I'll run right over and find Mr. Campbell."

There were still many last-minute jobs being hustled through. As soon as Orrin reached the strip of unkempt grass that ran between the two roughly parallel lines of brown canvas booths, he could hear the intermittent *tack-tack* of hammers. Men with shirt sleeves rolled up were knocking together counters and shelves or setting up displays of dolls and other prizes.

Luke Campbell, down on one knee unsnarling a heap of electric wire, looked up at Orrin with a smudged, perspiration-flooded face. "Drive around yonder by the fortune-teller's tent," he wheezed. "I'm fixing to have floodlights and a loud-speaker for you. Jess Tyndall is going to announce your act. You'll meet him presently."

"Swell," Orrin replied cheerfully, but the elaborateness of the preparations gave him a weak, shaky feeling.

Before Orrin backed Cloud from the trailer, he talked to her and patted her neck while she stood there trim and vital. "I'll give you a good going-over later and get rid of this dust," he promised.

Cloud tossed her head and pushed her soft, wrinkly muzzle over the side of the trailer. Orrin gave her a small chunk of carrot. Her strong white teeth closed on the tidbit with a contented crunch while Orrin stepped to the back of the trailer.

173

The place where Cloud was to perform was screened by a long row of trees, and the whole area had been roped off. Clara Martin walked along with Orrin while he led Cloud around the field. Several times the filly stopped and browsed leisurely at some spears of green grass.

"She's a good trouper," Mrs. Martin smiled. "She's not acting up."

"Not yet, anyway."

Around one o'clock Orrin and Clara sat in the shade of the trees and ate a sandwich while the palomino grazed near by. "You can keep Cloud hidden behind the pickup until I whistle for her," Orrin said to Mrs. Martin.

She agreed. "We'll get Luke to fasten a tarpaulin between the pickup cab and the trailer."

Orrin's misgivings about his outfit returned when he met Jess Tyndall. The first thing the announcer said was, "I'm not aiming to stick my big, old nose into your business, but what kind of get-up are you going to wear?"

"Just what I have on," Orrin replied. He could not keep the anxiety from his voice.

"Hm-m," the announcer mused, with a broad hand cupped over his chin. He was a rawboned man with shrewd blue eyes and a florid face. In spite of the hot sun, he was wearing a leather vest ornamented with silver. "This is your first show, isn't it?"

"Yes, sir."

"How did you get started on this trick horse deal?"

"In the first place, I guess it was because Cloud seemed to enjoy doing tricks. . . . And I liked being with her."

"Uh-huh—you Blacky's kin?"

Prompted by more questions, Orrin talked about himself until Jess Tyndall drawled, "Your story sounds plumb fascinating. We'll just forget about wearing fancy trappings. You carry on with your act just like you planned. I'll see you later."

Before it was time for Orrin to give Cloud her final burnishing, a set of loud-speakers along the carnival's midway began pouring out popular music. Orrin walked past the trees so that he could see what was happening.

The music was starting to draw a thin stream of fun seekers from the highway. Two small boys riding bareback on a sturdy chunk crossed the parking lot, followed by an open convertible full of noisy young men. The crowd was going to be a mixture of city and country people.

A glance at the concessions showed Orrin that the hotdog stand already had come customers. His gaze moved along the midway. All the booths were ready for business. From his detached position he could see how artificial the whole layout was. The entire accent was on sham and glitter. He compared it with the clean atmosphere of Sunset Hill and wondered what had drawn Luke Campbell to this kind of life.

Until it was time for their act, Orrin stayed with Mrs. Martin and Cloud. Luke Campbell, absent-mindedly gripping a small sledge hammer, had stopped by to see them for a minute.

"She sure looks ready," he said, with his narrow eyes still on the filly.

"Could you send over a tarpaulin?" Clara asked, and soon after Luke had hurried away, a man hung a tarpaulin where Mrs. Martin directed.

The noise and laughter beyond the trees grew less restrained. The carrousel ground out its tuneless music almost continuously, and the barkers raised their voices to a shriller pitch.

Jess Tyndall, walking backward, came from behind the fortune-teller's tent and unwound a coil of wire from around a microphone. When he reached the far side of the field, he called Orrin over. "Well," he said with a chuckle, "you raring to go?"

"I'm nervous," Orrin admitted. "How are we going to get started?"

"We'll wait until the folks fill up this section of chairs and then start the music. You'll stand by me until I tell you to march out to the middle of the field, and then I'll announce you. When that chore's attended to, you'll just naturally whistle for that pretty palomino of yours. Now, I reckon you better give me a list of your numbers."

Jess wrote down the tricks on the back of an envelope as Orrin gave them to him. "Be ready in about ten minutes," Jess said. He walked away, studying the envelope, and Orrin ran over for a last look at Coud.

He stroked her neck and crooned to her. She was a little restless, but became quiet as he talked.

"Will you stay right with her?" Orrin asked Mrs. Martin. "And would you mind running the rub rag over her? She likes that, and it will keep her coat shiny."

Suddenly all the music from the carnival stopped. Orrin found his lilac switch and then reached inside the pickup for a small parcel wrapped in wax paper. It held pieces of bread and carrots to reward Cloud for her tricks. He crammed this into his pocket as he went back to wait for Jess.

The loud-speakers came back to life all at once; somebody was making an announcement. A crawling tingle started up the back of Orrin's neck as he caught the words, "It's our feature attraction, folks. Orrin Toler and his incomparable palomino, Golden Cloud. Don't miss it, folks. Step to the far end of the grounds, friends . . ."

The crowd moved along good-naturedly and began to fill up the rows of folding chairs in front of Orrin. For the most part they were young couples on a day's outing.

A girl passing by looked back at her escort and laughed, "Just what is a palomino, Freddie?"

"This one is probably a washed-out buckskin. They always give them a big build-up at these carnivals."

Just then Jess Tyndall came up behind Orrin and drawled complacently, "There's a smart of people here for the first day. We'll have a good take."

All the seats were filled now and the latecomers were looking for places to stand. The loud-speakers made a crackling noise and the "Washington Post March" blared forth. Jess switched on the microphone beside him and let it warm up.

"Now," he said to Orrin. "Go right out there and wait for me to talk before you call Golden Cloud."

Orrin walked behind the noisy audience to the entrance and then straight out toward the center of the field. A man's amused voice behind him called, "Hey, Bub, you seen anything of a palomino?"

The remark brought a laugh from the spectators. Orrin held his head high and kept going on what seemed an endless journey. At last he stopped and turned around. He could feel his tongue thicken and his mouth go dry, and the fear that he would not be able to whistle struck him. A nervous glance toward the pickup showed that Clara Martin was keeping Cloud well hidden.

The music was cut off abruptly in the middle of a bar, and a fresh youngster shouted, "Don't just stand there, fellow. Do something."

Orrin tried to moisten his lips, and then Jess Tyndall's voice came softly but clearly over the public-address system. "Folks, our special feature this afternoon is a boy and his horse . . . Orrin Toler is just an ordinary lad, neighbors, who wandered into Oklahoma three years ago, hoping to find a home. And he found this with

Blacky and Clara Martin. Folks, there's nothing fancy-looking about this boy, but he has a gift with horses that is bestowed on few of the Lord's children."

Jess paused, there was not a sound anywhere on the field. Then his voice rang out again, "Ladies and gentlemen—with your permission—I present Orrin Toler and his palomino, Golden Cloud!"

The audience looked with one accord toward the lone figure in the field, leaned forward and applauded. A boy's shrill voice screamed through the noise, "Attaboy, Orrin!"

It took Orrin a moment to interpret the sudden change in the crowd. Then he understood. They were his friends! He suddenly relaxed, like an actor who has spoken his first lines and loses his nervousness. Facing the pickup, Orrin began to whistle sharply.

A gleam of light gold flashed in the sunlight and made everyone turn; then the people jumped to their feet. Golden Cloud, stretching out with her long, free stride, galloped across the field. The ripple of her magnificent mane and tail threw a glamour about her so that even the puffs of dust leaping up from her hoofs seemed to have the same golden color as her body.

She veered over to Orrin, slowed down and approached the boy with high, mincing steps. "Easy, Cloud," Orrin soothed softly. "Don't let the clapping bother you." As a reward, he held a piece of bread toward her and patted her forehead. He had to give her the command to kneel twice and strike her lightly on the knee with his switch, however, before she settled down and obeyed his orders.

Jess Tyndall injected a few comments as the act proceeded, but for the most part he let the pantomime of horse and master tell its own story. Cloud stood on her hind legs and pawed the air with her forefeet while

Orrin pretended they were boxing. She picked up Orrin's handkerchief and presented it to him. She lay down and rolled over, and when Orrin held up the act to brush the grass from her coat, the crowd cheered delightedly.

As the performance continued, Cloud began to understand the meaning of applause. It no longer distracted her. Instead, she put more zest into each trick, until Orrin laughed, "You like that clapping better than my carrots, don't you? I don't blame you. It sounds pretty good to me too," he added softly.

Near the end, when Orrin took his harmonica from his shirt pocket, Cloud was so eager that she could hardly stand still. When the music began, she tossed her head so happily as she danced that the response from the crowd was clamorous.

After the waltz ended, Orrin felt that he had made a mistake. This was where the act should stop, while the crowd's approval was at it height. He tried to think of some way to signal Jess, but the announcement was coming over the speakers:

"That was right pretty, folks, wasn't it? And it brings us to Golden Cloud's final number, a pose—a bit of living statuary—called *The Spirit of the Great Southwest*."

Orrin spoke into Cloud's cocked ear, "You've got to make this good." He wheeled her carefully until her full length was turned to the audience, and he gave her forelegs a light touch. She moved them forward, bracing her hind legs firmly. Her head arched higher with a bold tilt. Orrin ruffled her mane. He stood aside.

Cloud held herself motionless, each muscle under perfect control. It was difficult to tell if the crowd caught the beauty of her pose, for they were so quiet.

A long moment and then Orrin snapped his fingers. "Let's go," he said and started to run to the pickup, Cloud racing past him.

Orrin had nearly crossed the field when the applause came. Clapping, whistling, shouting, the noise rose louder and louder. It did not stop until Orrin managed to quiet Cloud enough to make her bow an encore.

"I'm right proud of you both," Clara Martin told Orrin when they reached the pickup.

"I am too," Orrin grinned. "Whew, it's hot! I forgot all about the weather."

They talked about the success until Mrs. Martin said reluctantly, "It's shameful to go home and leave you here until after tonight's show, but Blacky's no hand at milking cows, so I'd better go."

"We'll make out all right," Orrin replied, still grinning. "I've got a lot to talk over with Cloud . . . Oh, if you happen to see Barbara Johnson, tell her the show was O.K."

14. Tornado!

With the adeptness that comes from experience, Orrin swung the pickup and trailer in a wide arc from the highway to the carnival grounds. As the truck passed through the entrance, it stirred the air enough to make the pennants overhead dance feebly. Almost at once they sank back as limp and wilted as the concession men who sat outside their booths.

Orrin's face was sober, although he had tried his best to forget that Gabe Martin had been at Sunset Hill Ranch for the past two days. Gabe had been very much annoyed because Blacky had not turned Golden Cloud over to him at once, but the rancher refused to give his opinion of Gabe's chestnut filly until after the carnival ended.

Two of the men waved to Orrin as he drove past their booths, but the others did not even bother to look up.

They had little in common with this serious-looking boy who wanted to spend all his time with a horse.

It was Monday, just eight working days since the carnival had opened. Orrin parked in the usual place, rearranged the saddle and bridle that lay next to him in the pickup, and removed his shirt. He had an hour and a half before his act went on, but he wanted to take his time today. Even at eight o'clock that morning the temperature was one hundred degrees, and the breeze had died away completely. The consuming heat had given him a good excuse to get away from Gabe. While he pulled the tarpaulin over the pickup, the perspiration soaked through his trousers at his waist and above his knees.

The preceding days had been hot, but nothing like this. Orrin found a shady spot and began to groom Cloud. Later on, the swarthy woman who told fortunes would probably come over to steady Cloud until Orrin whistled. "We won't go riding between acts today," Orrin told Cloud as he brushed her. "That was all right while we had a breeze, but today we'll have a siesta—it's too hot to do any extra work!"

Orrin was giving Cloud a final rub with a handful of straw when Luke Campbell strolled over. "Your act has been a good drawing card," the promoter wheezed, as he laid a pudgy hand on Cloud's withers, but drew it back quickly as if he had touched something fragile. "I only wish the rest of the show had been as good."

Orrin caught a mournful expression in Luke's eyes. "What's the matter, Mr. Campbell?"

The wrinkles in Luke's forehead drew closer together, and he looked at Orrin solemnly. "I'm finding no fault with Golden Cloud, understand. In fact, I aim to go right on promoting you and her."

"I'm afraid that's out . . . What's wrong, Mr. Campbell? Isn't the carnival doing all right?"

"You've had the only paying proposition in the whole lot. We're folding, son."

Orrin's voice dropped. "When?"

"Five o'clock this evening. I've run a notice in the papers."

Only one more show! Orrin had not been prepared for this. He paid little attention to the other attractions at the carnival, but supposed they were all doing all right.

"I'll pay you presently," Luke went on. "You'll get every cent that's coming to you."

"Thanks," Orrin replied, slowly stroking Cloud with a handful of straw.

During the rest of the afternoon Orrin moved mechanically. Golden Cloud's tricks were well received, but Orrin noticed dully that the crowd was considerably smaller than it had been.

Luke Campbell was as good as his word. Before Orrin left for Sunset Hill, the promoter came to him with a green cash box and counted out three hundred and twenty-eight dollars and seventy-five cents. "That's correct to the penny," he said, resting the cash box on his knee as he swept a handkerchief over his dripping wet face. "And tell Blacky I'd like to get together with him about Golden Cloud's act. . . . You all take it easy now."

"Good-by, Mr. Campbell. I suppose—well, I guess this finishes things up."

"I reckon so," Luke replied. "Sometimes you win; sometimes you don't."

Orrin's hands lingered caressingly on Cloud as he led her into the trailer. "It's the last trip," he whispered to her as he banged the door shut.

At first Orrin drove slowly, for he was dejected by the sudden closing of the carnival. He had counted on having a few more days before Cloud would be taken away. There was no doubt in his mind what Blacky's decision would be. Gabe had the chestnut there at the ranch, and he talked with a confidence that could not have been assumed. Orrin had purposely stayed away from Gabe's filly, but he knew that she would be gentle and well trained. Gabe was skilful enough to know how to handle a horse right if he wanted to do it.

Gradually Orrin increased the speed of the pickup; if he hurried he could reach Sunset Hill in time for the milking. The engagement at the carnival had interrupted his routine at the ranch, and he had missed his regular chores. He would feel better when he got back on the job. The thought of working next to Clara in the dairy became more and more important. It had always been a pleasant duty to look forward to each day. And it was something to keep his mind on, something to depend on.

The inside of the pickup was very uncomfortable. The air moving between the open windows blew hot against his cheeks; the steering wheel almost burned his fingers. Everything he touched was the same. He looked at the sky and thought that it was not such a deep blue now as it had been all day. In spite of the rattle of the pickup, he could sense the disturbing quiet that lay about him.

Orrin knew of a dirt road that branched off to the right, farther along the highway. Clara Martin had pointed it out to him one time, and had told him it was a good short cut in dry weather. Orrin calculated quickly. If its surface was not rutted, it would get him to the ranch sooner, enough to make it worth trying.

When Orrin came to the dirt road, he took it without hesitation. The land on either side looked barren and unpopulated, but the road itself was fairly smooth, with enough room for another car to pass.

The road continued good, but the region that Orrin was passing through grew poorer. At first there had been scattered clumps of tall trees with shaggy, vine-covered trunks and sprays of mistletoe fanning out from the higher branches. These were behind him now. Low-growing bushes and jagged gullies had taken their place.

One of the pickup's cylinders missed firing several times, and Orrin began to wish that he had stayed on the main highway. He raised himself a little higher to look back at the trailer. Everything was all right there, but the sky behind it had taken on a dull, slate color. Cautiously he pressed his foot harder against the accelerator and listened to the motor.

The next time Orrin looked back, the sky was black just above the horizon. Intermittently the darkness was brightened by the glow of lightning.

"I ought to be getting back to the highway soon," Orrin muttered after he had traveled another five minutes. A shadow crossed the road and brought a gust of cooler air. Behind him the blackness had taken on a weird, greenish tinge. The dark wall crept higher into the sky, pushing clouds above it that eddied like gray smoke. Orrin thought to himself, "We're in for some fun." He laughed to reassure himself, but his voice had a nervous sound.

He had a general idea where he was now. The Frontier Club must be several miles behind and to the left. The storm was coming so slowly that there should be no trouble in staying ahead of it. To make sure of this, he fed the pickup a little more gas. The worn engine replied with a sputter and a sickly cough, recovered for a moment, and then stopped.

Several birds, flying low and swift, skimmed past on their way to shelter as the pickup and trailer rolled to the side of the road. But that was all the life Orrin could see. There was not even a squatter's shack to show that people lived anywhere in the locality.

The engine turned over when Orrin tried the starter, but it would not run. He got out of the cab and walked around to Cloud. The filly's sensitive ears were turned to the storm, and she stomped the floor of the trailer. Orrin patted her. "It's going to be a bad one when it comes."

A large portion of the sky was very dark now; eerie, with an added glow of copper. The sun would soon be hidden. "This road is going to be a river of red grease when that rain hits. For two cents I'd saddle you and get out of here while we still can."

An examination under the hood of the pickup showed that gas was flowing through to the carburetor as it should. There were no short circuits or loose connections. He began to think seriously of riding Cloud. The flare of lightning was becoming more vivid, and the thunder was continuous. Every moment it became plainer that the hot weather had built up a terrific disturbance in the atmosphere. Flash floods and impassable roads might hold the pickup there for days.

Orrin closed the hood and reached into the cab for the bridle. Cloud seemed reassured when she saw it and stood quietly while he slipped it on. Pad and saddle followed and then the filly, carrying Orrin, started down the road at a fast trot.

"We're not getting out of here any too soon," Orrin told Cloud. "I don't like the feel of the air. It's unnatural."

The tinted blackness that had been so slow in spreading began now to reach out faster toward the remaining blue sky. Within a few minutes the whole area was dark except when the lightning split it. A vast rush of air forced Orrin to bend in the saddle, and now he could hear the rain coming.

For about a mile Cloud kept her footing while the rain spilled down and lightning crackled close beside them. But the road was soaking up water fast and Cloud began to slip. Orrin drew her to a walk and tried to think what to do next; he could see that the filly was getting skittish. She started several times as if to bolt, but he held her back and steadied her. "What it is, girl?" he asked her. And then he saw something that frightened him.

Suddenly the rain slackened and the darkness began to lift as if it were clearing. Toward the west a ragged break appeared in the sky. But it only accentuated a densely black mass that held his gaze with the same kind of fascination that a snake wields over a helpless bird. Before the deadly, black funnel came into sight, Orrin knew that a tornado was whirling through the storm.

He could feel his muscles tighten. Some kind of protection was needed immediately . . . Wasn't there anything to turn to?

He glanced back apprehensively. A black shape, like a Dutchman's nightcap on end, snaked down from the cloud. It leaned crazily and bent back and forth with an undulating movement as it advanced. A blast of air, a distant moaning sound, and then a growing roar. He turned his gaze away and searched the region on either side of the road.

Over there across the ditch! The lightning pointed out a creek bed about seventy yards away, with high, sloping banks. A risky place to stay, he realized, but the best that was available. The water in it would not yet be deep. Instantly he threw the reins across Cloud's neck.

Cloud jumped the ditch with an effort and, finding more solid footing on the other side, leaped ahead without any signal from her rider. It was hard for Orrin to keep a seat in the wet saddle, but he managed somehow. They were approaching the brink of the stream when Cloud struck a treacherous spot. As she stumbled, Orrin felt himself lifted from the saddle. Lightning seemed to explode in his brain and then there was darkness.

Water everywhere. Water that oozed over his face and choked off his breathing. Orrin's thoughts fluttered weakly for a moment. He tried to move his head and felt the sucking sound of mud against one cheek. Now he was conscious of the slap of rain against the other side of his face.

Slowly he drew his knees under him and started to rise. Then his head came up with a jerk, and he was completely alert. Where was Cloud?

It was still raining hard, although the extreme darkness had passed. Orrin looked anxiously in every direction, but Cloud was nowhere in sight. He whistled as loudly as he could and waited tensely for an answering nicker. Again and again he whistled until he realized it was useless.

"Don't get panicky," Orrin warned himself. "The tornado couldn't have come this way, or I wouldn't be here. Cloud probably was frightened and kept running for a while. She must have left some tracks."

Bending low, he walked slowly back and forth, searching the muddy ground. All he could find were two puddles near the place where he had been lying. These might have been left by hoofs, but the rain had destroyed all signs of a trail.

A loud gurgling made him look toward the creek. Water had risen halfway up its banks. He must have lain unconscious for some time. Cloud would not have tried to cross the stream; she must have gone in the opposite direction. He plodded through the mud to the road and walked along the edge of the flooded ditch looking for hoof marks. Nothing there. He followed the ditch for about a hundred feet and stopped. The road was littered with broken branches, leaves, splintered boards, a fence post, and some tangled wire. Orrin stared at the heap with a worried frown. The tornado had barely missed him, but where was Cloud?

Perhaps the filly had run in the other direction. If so, it was possible that she had reached the highway and found her way back to the ranch. Orrin whistled, straining to make the sound carry through the rain. "There is only one thing to do," he thought at last. "I'll walk home and see if Cloud is there."

Absent-mindedly, as if it did not matter, Orrin felt the thick wad of bills in his pocket. It was no use trying to keep them dry. They would have been soaked by now no matter where he had put them.

Orrin kept going, sliding as he went, the red mud clinging to his riding boots until they became heavy, shapeless lumps. At intervals he whistled, but no filly appeared. When at last he came to the main highway, he stopped long enough to pry the mud from his boots with a sharp stick and then he strode on.

The highway bridge near the ranch was lost under a tawny spread of water that had backed up the highway like a small lake. Orrin transferred the soggy mass of paper money to his shirt pocket, pulled off his boots and socks, and began to wade. He paused with the water tugging against his knees and gave another forlorn whistle. There was little chance that Cloud had come through at that spot. The water must be waist-deep in the middle, and maybe the bridge had been washed away.

Cautiously Orrin felt his way along, bracing himself against the flood and advancing a few inches at a time. When he judged that he was at the bridge, the water was curling above his belt and he could feel an insistent lift from the current.

He was over now; the bridge was still holding. But he did not step freely until he was in shallow water. When he put his boots on again, they were uncomfortably tight. He could feel the sting of raw blisters on the back of his heels, but there was no thought of stopping.

Orrin hurried on, limping as the pain from the blisters became worse. Finally he could see the Martins' mailbox ahead of him. He peered up the hillside into the rain and whistled. Cloud did not appear. Now he was picking his way up the drive, avoiding the gullies that had been carved there. Something strange caught his attention; behind the ranch house a dozen pecan trees lay in tangled heaps, their leaves stripped off the branches. A jagged path, bare in places, scattered with debris in others, crossed the field near the dairy. The tornado must have struck Sunset Hill!

Another glance at the house reassured him; it had not been touched. A little farther, and he could see that the red barn had not been damaged either. Cloud might be in there right now.

"Mrs. Martin!" Orrin shouted to the house. "Blacky!" He paused a moment and then cut back toward the dairy. If the tornado had ripped through the cow barn, Clara Martin's entire herd was lost.

He reached the top of the path and looked downhill apprehensively. But the cow barn was standing. The track of the tornado was spotty here. Pump house, milkhouse, the small buildings seemed the same as ever.

As Orrin watched, Blacky's face, under a dripping felt hat, appeared at the door of the milkhouse. He stepped into the rain and went around the far side of the building. His wife started out the door to accompany him.

"Hello!" Orrin called.

Clara saw him and looked up in surprise. She exclaimed, "Now, how did Luke know enough to send you home?" Then she saw his bedraggled clothing and uneven gait. "Orrin, you're limping. Are you hurt?"

"I'm all right," Orrin said, "but Cloud—didn't she come back?"

Clara shook her head slowly as Blacky called back from

the far side of the milkhouse, "Look here, Clara, the tool shed's gone."

Orrin followed behind Clara and stared at the empty spot where the tool house had stood. The building, used for storing odd pieces of furniture, had been built as an addition to the milkhouse. By its freak action, the tornado had ripped off the tool shed, leaving the wall of the milkhouse in perfect condition.

Orrin forgot momentarily about Cloud while his mind struggled with this strange happening. As he stood there, weary and puzzled, he caught sight of a large white object leaning against the trunk of a cottonwood tree fifty yards away.

"Oh," he thought as recognition came, "that's the old refrigerator that used to be in the tool shed! . . . Boy, a tornado sure does have force. We're really lucky to get off so easy."

15. A Bitter Decision

THREE full days had passed since Golden Cloud's disappearance, and not a trace of her had been found. The police continued to watch all highways in Oklahoma and adjoining states, but neither they nor the newspapers had produced a single lead. Blacky had called Sim Remy, the president of the Frontier Club, for help in searching the back country. Thirty members of the club, on horseback, had fanned out over the whole region and covered it rod by rod, but with no success.

Clara Martin was the only person at Sunset Hill whose spirit was stanch enough to endure the strain. The others had become jumpy and irritable. Orrin spoke less than anyone, but his eyes were dark and shadowy. It wasn't only that Blacky had conceded Gabe's filly to be perfectly trained and mannered; even worse than that was the uncertainty about Cloud. She might be lying somewhere at that very moment, waiting for help to come.

Although Blacky had reluctantly agreed with Gabe that further search by horseback was useless, Orrin would not give up. In this determination he was earnestly supported by Barbara Johnson.

It was just before dawn of the fourth day following the tornado. Overhead the stars were still throwing their white light across endless black space. In the dimness, two riders jogged along the dirt road toward the place where the pickup lay temporarily abandoned. Orrin, riding Buck, and Barbara on Spice, were off on another day's hunt for the lost palomino.

"Let's start this side of the pickup today and ride southwest," Orrin suggested heavily.

"Good idea. That's the roughest country around here . . . You're tired, aren't you, Orrin? If we don't find anything today, you better stay home tomorrow and rest."

"Not me. I'll keep looking until Cloud is found."

"I know how you feel. But, Orrin, there's a limit to what you can take."

The thud of hoofs filled the next mile. One by one the stars gave a final blink and withdrew behind a gray canopy.

"The sun's coming up," Barbara said, glancing at the thin streaks in the eastern sky. "You know, Orrin, I have a feeling that Cloud is going to turn up today."

"That would be good news for Gabe."

Barbara's voice was suddenly petulant. "Wasn't that a low-down trick of Gabe's to train his filly so carefully? He doesn't really think any more of a horse's feelings now than he ever did."

"He says he does."

193

"Well, there's something strange about it. Orrin, are you sure it's the same filly he started with?"

Orrin straightened quickly and looked at her. "How could we tell?"

"What about that tiny white patch on her flank—remember?"

"Yeah!" Orrin said slowly. "I don't think it's there now." Then he slumped back on the saddle. "I don't know what difference it makes, if we don't find Cloud."

All day long Buck and Spice carried their riders over a desolate stretch that had been scored by the recent storm. It was the kind of region where an injured horse could waste away without anyone's finding her.

Orrin and Barbara traveled back and forth, riding about a hundred feet apart, methodically searching acre after acre. Twice they investigated grimly when they saw buzzards circling in the sky. But the ugly birds had been attracted by nothing larger than dead rodents.

At nightfall, when they abandoned the search, Orrin said, "We'll start here tomorrow and go on beyond those scrub pines."

Barbara was tired and her face was scratched, but she nodded gamely. "I'll meet you the same time. Orrin, I'm so tired I could go to sleep in the saddle, but I'm going to stop at Sunset Hill on the way home and look at the filly."

When Orrin and Barbara reached the ranch, Clara was waiting by the back porch. Orrin shook his head wearily to show Mrs. Martin they had had no luck.

"Too bad," Mrs. Martin said. "You go right in and get to bed, Orrin. I'll take care of Buck."

"Thanks. I'm not that bad off. We're going to take a look at the chestnut. Is Gabe around?"

"No, he isn't. But Barbara's dad sent his man Charley over to help us out. He's somewhere around the stable now, I reckon. He'll know where Gabe's filly is. Barbara, it was right neighborly of your folks to help us out."

Barbara's eyes shone in the spread of light from the kitchen window. "That's all right, Mrs. Martin. Dad was probably glad to get rid of Charley. He's just a worthless old codger."

"About as worthless as a gold nugget," Clara declared, and Barbara gave an emphatic nod of her head.

Charley was coming out of the barn toward the tractor when Barbara saw him and asked about Gabe's horse.

"Thisaway," Charley said laconically, and then led the way to a corner of the pasture.

"Which side was that white patch on?" Orrin asked Barbara as they walked along in the increasing darkness.

Barbara thought a moment. "The left. I'm sure it was."

The chestnut stood quietly while they approached. Charley stood at her head and patted her while Orrin and Barbara bent their heads close to her body.

"Nothing here but a brand," Orrin muttered. "No white hair."

Barbara studied the mark as best she could in the darkness. "A terrible job of branding. Look at the size of it." She walked around to the other side. "Nothing at all here."

"You think that brand could have burned off the patch?"

Barbara was thoughtful. "Could be."

Charley, who had said nothing up until now, spoke up. "That Gabe's no good. His filly don't like him."

"You don't think so, Charley?"

"He's no good," Charley grunted.

Barbara and Orrin and Charley walked back from the pasture. "Why don't you write to the ranch where Gabe works and ask the owner about this chestnut?" Barbara suggested.

"Yeah—all right. That's not a bad idea. I suppose Mrs. Martin has the address."

"I mean it, Orrin. Write tonight. Promise?"

"Yes, I will."

Barbara turned to Charley. "I am going to help Orrin again tomorrow."

"We'll all help," Charley said stolidly.

"I mean we're going to ride again."

"Good. You ride; I'll come here."

Before Orrin dragged himself into bed, he wrote a brief note to the ranch in Texas. He asked Mrs. Martin sleepily, "Would you mind mailing this letter in the morning? And if you see Gabe tomorrow, ask him what happened to that little white patch on his filly's near flank."

"I'll do that. Now you get off to bed."

Before sunrise the next morning Orrin was out of the house. He stopped at the tack room and gathered up his saddle and bridle and carried them out into the darkness. A pungent, leathery smell filled the air he was breathing, but it had become so much a part of his life that he hardly noticed it.

After considerable fumbling, he drew the saddle snug on Buck and rode out the driveway.

Barbara was waiting by the mailbox, an obscure outline in the darkness. She welcomed Orrin with a brief "Hey."

"Hello," Orrin replied. "Am I late?"

"No. I just got here. Want a sandwich? I made a couple of extra ones."

"Thanks."

They rode on together, the air brushing moistly against their faces. "I hope we have good luck today," Barbara said.

At the end of an hour the screens of gray mist slid

apart, revealing a panorama that ended in a wide sweep of blue sky. While the sun started its steep morning climb, Buck and Spice ranged systematically through the scrub pines.

Far beyond the pine land the search continued until finally the sun had dropped so far down in the west that they had to turn back.

"Tomorrow morning?" Barbara asked when they reached Sunset Hill.

"Yes—the same time." Orrin shifted laboriously in the saddle. He had not been hardened to so much riding. "Gee, Barbara, I'm beginning to wonder—"

"What, Orrin?"

"Skip it. I'll see you in the morning."

Orrin's whole body throbbed from one great, engulfing ache as he rode into the ranch. At the back porch he looked for Mrs. Martin, but she was not there. It was the first time she had failed to meet him. He frowned at the dark kitchen and tried not to admit the hopelessness of riding out day after day. "Come on. Get along," he muttered to Buck as they rode toward the barn.

A light shone from the barn window at the end of the stalls. Orrin was wondering about this when he saw Mrs. Martin coming along the opposite side of the driveway.

"It's you, Orrin. I was on my way to meet you." Clara Martin looked up at his face and then down again. "We were late doing the chores. Charley had to go to the city for Ike Johnson and didn't get here until after dinner. He stayed right with us, though. He's yonder at the barn now."

"He's a nice fellow."

"He sure is; but don't stop to help him. You need your sleep."

Orrin rode the tough little buckskin to the paddock and

was watering him when Charley stepped quietly along-side them.

"Hello," Orrin said, expecting no more than a grunt from Ike Johnson's hired man. But there was an alertness about the usually stolid Charley that could be seen even in this poor light.

"You didn't find the palomino," Charley said.

"No."

"If you find her, Blacky will give her to Gabe?"

"Yes, that's right."

"Then why do you want to find her?"

Orrin was utterly weary, and Charley's persistence irritated him. He answered gruffly, "Maybe she's—suffering."

"Gabe's no good," Charley said doggedly. "His own horse don't like him."

"You've said that before," Orrin cried. "That's not the point."

Charley gave an approving grunt at the boy's show of temper. His shoulder touched Orrin's. He said in a whisper, "I found out something today. The palomino wasn't hurt."

"What!" Orrin exclaimed. "How do you know?"

"I know." Charley spoke the words proudly. "We all helped look for Golden Cloud. My people; my wife's people, Marie's cousin found her—"

"Cloud? Where is she?"

"Strong young horses can run far. We'll leave her with Marie's cousin until Gabes goes away."

"But Blacky promised—"

Charley squeezed Orrin's arm. "You want Gabe to have the palomino? His own horse don't—"

"Have you told anyone? Would anyone know?" There was a tremor in Orrin's voice. Maybe it could be done. With Charley's help the secret could be kept. It wasn't as if Gabe had earned Cloud honestly . . . But he *had* won her honestly. All Charley's talk about the chestnut's not liking Gabe had nothing to do with the bargain. "Charley, I don't know what to do."

Charley spoke roughly, "That Gabe's no good. I won't tell anybody about finding Golden Cloud."

"I'll think it over," Orrin said miserably, "and let you know."

In the shadow of the barn Charley shook his head impatiently at Orrin's indecision. He muttered something about Gabe and stalked away.

Orrin started after him, hesitated, and called, "Charley, tell Barbara I'm staying home tomorrow."

As Orrin left the paddock, his thoughts struggled against one another. Whenever any one idea seemed about to rise above the others, it was pulled back and churned under again.

"I could try leaving Cloud where she is," he thought. "Then I could get out to her once in a while. I'd give anything to see her shining in the sunshine. To feel her smooth coat. And the way she comes flying up when I whistle . . .

"What would Mrs. Martin do if she were in my place? Probably tell Blacky and Gabe. Why did Blacky ever make such a stupid agreement? Gabe never did take care of a horse right, and never will. He must have been good to that chestnut, though . . . I wonder if I'll hear anything from that ranch in Texas?

"Oh, shucks, the sooner Gabe gets Cloud and the whole business is settled, the better. I might as well tell everybody right away. Nobody could ever be cruel to a filly like Cloud. But when I think about Gabe and the way Cloud always trusted me . . ."

Orrin went to bed that night without telling the Martins that he was not going to look for Cloud in the morning. A half-admitted plan lay in the back of his mind. He could get up at the same hour tomorrow and go right to Cloud. The desire to be with her again struck him like a fever. During the days that he had been searching for her his feelings had been numb; he had not dared to hope for anything. Now that she had been found, he was flung between elation and bitterness.

"I'll go and see Cloud before I make up my mind about the rest," Orrin told himself, and rolled over to go to sleep. But he began to toss. Should he tell Barbara? He tossed around again. It was too warm in the room to sleep. After all, Cloud belonged to Blacky, and Orrin had no right to hide her. What was it that Uncle Chauncey had always said—you must think of yourself first. But that wasn't the way Mrs. Martin had treated him.

When he finally went to sleep, the same thoughts were there, only distorted out of all proportion, and twice he awoke himself with his own muttering. Before daylight he awoke again and looked upward with dry, aching eyes. He lay there thinking until he heard Blacky and Clara go downstairs. Then he got up and dressed. He listened, but there was no sound from the spare room, where Gabe slept.

When Orrin walked into the kitchen, Blacky's hand was raising a cup of coffee. His hand paused abruptly, and Blacky studied Orrin through a wisp of steam.

Clara glanced back from an open cabinet and her gray eyes warmed pleasantly. "I was hoping you'd stay home for a day and rest."

"It seemed like the best thing to do." Orrin was not facing Blacky, but he could feel the rancher's shrewd inspection. It brought a self-conscious flush to his cheeks. "Maybe I'll give up looking altogether."

After a little while, Orrin could sense that the rancher was no longer staring at him. He wished that Blacky would say something to show what he was thinking. Orrin sat down awkwardly and reached for a cereal dish and a spoon.

Mrs. Martin looked from Blacky to Orrin. She said to her husband, "You get started on the chores and I'll fry some bacon for Orrin."

"All right," Blacky replied. He finished the coffee and left the room.

Orrin ate his cereal with little appetite while Clara cut some strips of bacon.

"You go back to bed after breakfast," Mrs. Martin said kindly.

Orrin examined the pattern around the edge of his dish for a moment and then abruptly pushed back his chair and stood up. He walked to the outside door and stared moodily through the glass pane.

"I've got something I have to tell you," he said, turning to Mrs. Martin.

"Yes, Orrin."

"Mrs. Martin, you probably never felt the way I do. You always know what's right and what to do and—"

"Nobody is always sure, Orrin."

"I mean you wouldn't kick around all night trying to make something seem right that wasn't. Or maybe it was right and you weren't sure. Oh, what the heck . . . Mrs. Martin, I know where Cloud is."

"You do! Why, Orrin! M-m-m—I see."

"Well—what would you do in my place?"

"You mean about telling Blacky and Gabe?"

"Yes."

Mrs. Martin did not reply immediately, and Orrin could not force himself to stand still any longer. A fierce restlessness drove him back to the table. He stood behind a chair and began rocking it from side to side.

Mrs. Martin brought a dish of curling, brown bacon to

the table and set it in front of Orrin. "Sit down and eat it while it's hot," she said.

Orrin obeyed her and looked at the bacon. Mrs. Martin sat down next to him.

Orrin reached for a fork. "Is Gabe around?"

"He's upstairs. Won't be down for a good long while . . . Orrin, I'd like to tell you what to do, but I'm not going to."

Orrin ran his left hand wearily through his hair. He let the fork slide from his other hand and lean against the plate.

"It wouldn't be right for me to try to tell you what to do, Orrin. You'll have to decide for yourself what's best. You're old enough to do that."

"But I don't know what's best; that's the trouble." Orrin's mouth twisted at one side.

Mrs. Martin looked at him sympathetically, but there was a firmness there that Orrin understood. It was the first time she had ever deserted him. He was cut away from his one strong support—adrift again. The savor of bacon made his stomach tighten unpleasantly.

"O.K. Thanks, anyway." He got to his feet without looking at her and started outdoors.

"I won't repeat a word to anybody," Clara said.

Orrin's way led inevitably to the barn. His tired brain could not hold any single thought long enough to examine it. But thoughts formed into patterns, and the patterns aroused emotions that burned with dull heat.

The barn had never felt so empty. The smell of gasoline and hay passed by him, and then there was the smell of the stable. A whiff of leather took him past the open tack room, and then he leaned on the lower half of the door to the box stall.

Orrin's thoughts turned all the way back to those last days in China—the fever and hushed voices; the emptiness that followed his father's and mother's deaths . . .

A poignant resolve came to him. He must not permit Cloud to leave him the way the others did.

"Orrin! Orrin! Are you there?"

He raised his head with a jerk and looked around, startled.

The slatted door scraped open and Barbara Johnson appeared at the end of the passageway.

"Hello," Orrin called.

"I thought I'd find you here." The eager glow in her wide, brown eyes was blended with the old self-consciousness. She stumbled once as she approached. "Charley told me you wouldn't be going today."

"No." Orrin looked back into the empty stall.

"Orrin, you mustn't let this get you down. I feel surer than ever that Cloud is safe somewhere."

A guilty feeling made Orrin's breath jump. Had Charley told her about finding Cloud? No, he guessed he hadn't. But it was really a mean trick to let Barbara go on talking and not say anything.

In her effort to encourage Orrin, Barbara seemed like the ungraceful youngster of two years ago. "Why don't you get a good rest today, and we'll leave a half-hour earlier tomorrow. The horses will be good and fresh too, and—"

"Do you think we ought to keep looking?"

"Of course! We can't give up so easily."

"Easily—"

"Orrin, you need something else to think about." She hesitated and seemed about to give the quick, backward toss of her head that had been her habit when she wore pigtails. But something seemed to steady her, and when she spoke, her poise had returned. "We're having a party two weeks from tomorrow night and we want you and Clara and Blacky to come. There will be dancing—"

"Party!" Orrin did not try to keep the bitterness from his voice.

"Yes." A quiet strength gave depth to her voice. "Whatever happens, it's not going to help you any to brood over it."

Orrin had the uncomfortable feeling that Barbara had grown up faster than he had. He leaned over the door and pretended to adjust the latch, all the while his moodiness increasing. A sudden flush of exasperation tingled all the way to his ears. He was like an animal in a tight corner. The next thing, Barbara would remind him that he was nineteen years old. After she went home, he would find a way to get to Cloud. Take the filly and leave Sunset Hill for good—that was the only way.

Barbara talked a little longer and began backing to the door. "I'll meet you in the morning?"

"No, I'm not going."

"I'll be at the mailbox anyway, in case you change your mind." She paused and smiled, as if hoping he would start to talk.

But Orrin's only reply was a stubborn shake of his head. After she left, he scowled at the place where she had been.

The rumble of the barn door, closing behind Barbara, brought a feeling of repentance to Orrin. He shouldn't have been so surly with her. She was only trying to be friendly. Well, it was too late to do anything about it now.

He looked inside the tack room. Everything was out of order. Between Charley and Gabe, they had managed to make a mess out of the place. Roughly he began putting things where they belonged. As soon as he could think a little straighter, he would hunt up Charley and find out where Cloud was.

Orrin threw open the outside door of the tack room

and began sweeping the floor. The golden figure of a palomino in varying sizes and poses glimmered in front of the broom. He closed his eyes to shake away the images. Before he resumed sweeping, he heard men talking in the paddock outside the door.

In a moment he recognized Gabe's voice, raised angrily. "You all aiming to throw me out like an old boot. Well, I'm not asking for anything that isn't mine. If you want me to go, why don't you give me the palomino?"

"Didn't say I wouldn't give her to you—if I had her." The voice belonged to Blacky.

"You're hiding her. You put that fool kid up to it."

"Don't talk thataway." Blacky's voice was curt.

"You and your promises," Gabe said scornfully. "And I acted in good faith, thinking you meant it."

Inside the tack room Orrin tried to make up his mind whether to go outdoors or to step into the barn. He couldn't stand there spying on the two men.

"Tell you what I'll do." Blacky's voice had a solemn ring that held Orrin against his will. "If Golden Cloud doesn't show up by the end of the week, I'll give you Queen."

There was silence outside. Orrin gasped as he realized the sacrifice that Blacky was offering to make.

When Gabe's voice replied, it could not mask his greed and excitement. "It's a deal! I'll take her and that'll be the last you'll ever see of me."

"It's a deal," Blacky said thickly.

Scarcely breathing, Orrin stole through the inner door of the tack room and closed it quietly behind him. When the chance came, he retreated unseen to the house and into his bedroom. There he stayed right through the usual dinner hour, presumably resting.

Blacky's offer to give away Queen had shocked Orrin and changed the course of his thinking. He had realized immediately that he could not keep Cloud hidden now, nor could he run away with her. That last thought had been a crazy idea anyway. His feeling of frustration and anger at Blacky had died away slowly. During the course of the day he had grown more thoughtful. It might even be a good thing that Blacky had acted as he did.

There was no longer anybody for Orrin to turn to for advice, but within his own mind a certain order was developing. He was discovering a new power within himself to think through the situation. It came to him clearly that Clara Martin had acted with wisdom when she had refused to tell him what to do. He stretched out on his stomach across the foot of the bed and stared at the cows in the east pasture.

The shadows moving along with the cows began to stretch farther down the hillside. The herd started nosing in the direction of the cow barn.

Orrin swung his feet around to the floor and leaned over to put his shoes on. If he hurried, he could see Blacky before milking time. His fingers moved more quickly as he tied his shoelaces. It was almost going to be like getting back into the old routine. But the hardest part was just before him.

He found Blacky walking up the back path to the house, hugging a big watermelon. The rancher said, "I've been tapping this fellow every day for a week, and now its ready."

In the sober cheerfulness of this remark Orrin caught a clear glimpse into the durable fiber of Blacky's character. It was hard to believe that this man had consented only this morning to give away a horse that he considered beyond value. Blacky was really one great guy. The discord that had tormented Orrin's mind during the past few years smoothed out even more. He wasn't going to feel like whistling and shouting, but neither was he going to sulk. Blacky had shown how a man with courage could act, and that was a good enough example to follow.

"Blacky . . ."

"Yes."

"I have a confession to make."

"Wait," Blacky said in an alarmed voice. He stopped and laid the melon on the ground. "I don't want to hear it." He gave his head an earnest shake.

"You've got to, Blacky. I know where Cloud is."

Blacky did not reply. His face slowly turned downward, and he seemed to be contemplating the melon. He displayed neither anger nor joy. "You shouldn't have told me," he said.

"You mean you knew the secret?"

"We both love our horses, Orrin. I couldn't help but guess what happened when you stayed home today. I been trying hard not to—know it."

Orrin did not dare trust his voice for a moment. Blacky had actually planned to give away Queen so Gabe would not get Cloud. The hillside spun dizzily while Orrin tried to comprehend this. He had never guessed that Blacky felt that way toward him.

Blacky went on gloomily as if it were a disappointment to know that Queen was staying. "I've watched you and Cloud grow up together. Many a time I've wanted to give myself the quirt for making that deal with Gabe. But, Orrin, a promise is a promise and has to be kept."

"That's right," Orrin said levelly.

"I could see you and Cloud together the day I chased Caldwell's dog. I reckon that was when I knew she was your filly. After that I was aiming to save her for you— little thinking Gabe would make good."

"That's all right," Orrin said. "You were only doing what you thought best."

"Thanks, pardner." He picked up the watermelon and started walking.

Orrin understood all that Blacky meant by calling him pardner. That was how he talked to a man.

"I'll go and get Cloud tomorrow," Orrin said, and his voice was steady.

16. A Promise Is Fulfilled

IKE JOHNSON's Ford sedan was rolling briskly toward Oklahoma City. An empty horse trailer pushed against the back of the Ford as if urging it to even greater speed. Charley was driving the car; next to him sat Orrin.

"That Gabe," Charley muttered after a long silence, "he's no—"

"Yeah, I know," Orrin interrupted hurriedly, and Charley subsided.

A long ride faced the two. They planned to travel in a great half-circle in order that Charley could attend to some business for his boss in the city. Eventually they would reach the obscure ranch where Cloud was waiting.

As anxious as Orrin was to see Cloud, he was satisfied to take the long way to reach there. Their meeting would be no more than the beginning of a farewell. Orrin understood this; he had tried to condition his mind to it, but the filly would think it was a reunion. This troubled Orrin more than anything else. If only Cloud knew what had happened, she and Orrin could meet each other with outward cheerfulness—the way a soldier on his last furlough might greet his friends at home. But not for a moment did Orrin wish that Blacky were going for Cloud instead of himself.

When they reached Oklahoma City, Charley drove across a bridge over the railroad tracks and parked at the edge of the business section. "Staying in the car?" he asked Orrin.

Orrin considered a short time. "No," he said abruptly, "I'm going to take a look at the stores. I'll meet you back here."

When Orrin returned, he had half a dozen slices of bread wrapped in waxpaper, and an oblong box. His taciturn companion watched him lay the box on the back seat with no signs of curiosity, and Orrin made no explanation.

The sedan and trailer recrossed the bridge, followed the highway and then took to dirt roads, working their way south and west. Now and again Orrin felt an excitement swell inside him, and leaned forward on the seat. Each time, by stubborn will power, however, he subdued his eagerness and settled back.

The film of dust on the hood of the car gradually thickened; the windshield got dirtier. Every rutty mile they passed the land grew poorer—first an abandoned shack and later the ruins of one-time houses.

Charley looked at the narrow road. "If we meet another car, somebody backs up," he grunted.

They came to an unkempt tract where gaunt-ribbed

cattle occasionally poked their way out from between bushes. "About half mile more," Charley said.

Orrin's breath gave a quick flutter, but he nodded his head stoically. "Blacky will take care of giving your cousin a reward," he said.

"John's ranch," Charley announced, when they could see patches of brown grass between the bushes. He steered into a cluttered yard where two goats were grazing in front of an unpainted shack. When they spied the car, a woman and two small children fled from the rotting porch into the house closing the door as far as it would go on its broken hinges.

Charley paid no attention to them, but sat in the car and blew the horn steadily until a swarthy man lumbered from behind the house.

"John, we came for the palomino," Charley called with a certain importance that showed he was a person of consequence at this place.

"Sure," John answered. He was a hulking fellow, obviously lacking in ambition. "She's in the barn."

Orrin walked toward the barn with a kind of light-headedness, a queer feeling that he was someone else. He wanted to whistle toward that shapeless gray building, but that would not have been fair to Cloud. They must meet casually.

Charley was saying something to John about the reward, Orrin knew. John dragged a door back against a pile of manure and led the way inside the barn. A questioning whinny rang through the dimness. Orrin could not hold back another minute; he whistled.

A shrill outburst answered him. That was really Cloud he knew now. Orrin ran the length of the barn to a stall at the other end.

It was a rank-smelling stall, and the filly was fighting the rope that held her. Orrin cried, "Cloud, take it easy!" as he stood back from the frantic animal. "Cloud! Cloud!" he cried, half-laughing, half-scolding.

Golden Cloud quieted down except for low, excited cries that she could not hold back in her chest. Orrin squeezed into the stall alongside her. All the calmness that he had forced upon himself had vanished. He threw his arms around her neck and hugged her. He was trembling as much as the filly.

"You're going to get a lot of grooming the very first thing," Orrin promised her. It was the one thought he dared to concentrate on. Cloud did need grooming; from the looks of her caked hair and snarled mane she had not been touched since the day of the tornado.

Orrin untied her and led her from the barn. The sound of her hoofs on the hard earth floor was like part of himself that had returned. Cloud stepped nervously under the open sky, danced skittishly at a locust's whirring song close by. Orrin talked to her and patted her neck, which was shamefully dull now like the rest of her body.

It took time to coax Cloud into the trailer, but Orrin succeeded. He noticed with relief that her nostrils had stopped quivering and that her eyes had steadied. "They didn't starve you. That's one good thing," Orrin told her. He clung to the side of the trailer, knowing all the time that it was the wrong thing to do.

"I'll be back," he said suddenly, for he had remembered the slices of bread in the car. This gave him a perfect excuse to spend a few more minutes with Cloud.

When at last Charley guided the car out of the yard, Orrin leaned his cheek on his hand and sat with half-closed eyes.

"That palomino sure glad to see you," Charley chuckled. "She's your—"

"Oh, stop it!" Orrin cried. He did not realize how curtly

he had spoken, even after Charley gave him a sidelong look.

Charley kept quiet after that, and Orrin hardly moved while the sedan traveled toward Sunset Hill. Once he looked around at Cloud. Seeing that she was riding quietly, he was satisfied, and turned back to look at the scenery.

He was now conscious of familiar landmarks, a broken windmill, a concrete bridge. The miles rushed past with bewildering speed. It had promised to be a long trip, and here he was already looking at the pecan grove at Sunset Hill Ranch.

A short climb at a slow pace and the car stopped. Charley sat patiently waiting until Orrin came to with a muffled "Oh" and realized he was at the ranch house.

Cloud snuffed the air excitedly and pointed her sensitive ears forward and back. She stretched her neck and whinnied joyfully. Orrin hastened to back her from the trailer before her excitement became too great. He clung to her and calmed her while, with arched head and tail, she pranced up the driveway.

At the palomino's first whinny Clara Martin had run to the back porch, where she stood quietly and watched the two. When Orrin finally saw her, she smiled and came closer. Cloud was standing still now, her muzzle at Orrin's shoulder. She was alert to every sensation that told her she was home again, but attentive to Orrin, above all else.

Mrs. Martin stroked Cloud's lusterless back. "She's sorry-looking now, Orrin, but it's only dirt. She's as sound as ever."

"That's right . . . I'm going to take her down to the paddock and give her a good grooming."

Charley started to drive past them, but stopped almost immediately and reached into the back seat. "You forgot this," he said, holding up the package Orrin had bought in the city.

"Oh, thanks," Orrin said, as he glanced quickly at Mrs. Martin.

"I'll hold Cloud while you get it," she said.

Orrin got the package and looked about for a place to lay it. "I guess I'd better put it in the house," he said and turned, without waiting for a reply.

Orrin ran through the kitchen and upstairs to his room. He placed the package in a dresser drawer. When he straightened up, he saw a letter lying on top of the dresser. A quick, careless glance—and then a rapid throbbing of his pulse. It was a reply from the ranch in Texas!

He ripped open the envelope and unfolded the letter. All sounds in the room were suspended as he started to read. He stopped after the first two sentences and closed his eyes tight for a moment. His hands, still holding the paper, dropped limply to his sides. Then he thrust the letter into his pocket and started slowly down the stairs. The chestnut filly was actually the same horse that Gabe had bought as a foal. And it was also true that Gabe had erased the white patch with his brand. Well . . . it really would have been foolish to expect anything different.

Clara Martin must have misunderstood Orrin's expression when he returned to the driveway. "Blacky isn't home," she began. "He made Gabe go away until tomorrow, and then he himself began getting right upset. I reckon he just couldn't standing being here when—"

"I know what you mean," Orrin interrupted. "Blacky is the greatest guy in the world. Here, I'll take Cloud now."

"Blacky went over to Ike Johnson's. He'll know you're back when he sees Charley."

Orrin turned Cloud loose in the paddock so she could enjoy a run, but she refused to leave him. Instead, she stayed right at his side while he walked toward the tack room door. "You haven't forgotten me, have you?" Orrin asked her. "Remember the day—" His voice broke off, and he looked hard at the side of the barn. "What you need right now is a good bath."

He got a bucket and a brush from the tack room. As he washed away the grime from her coat, he thought that the richness of her contrasting gold and silver held greater beauty than ever before.

It was hard for him to keep from planning revenge against Gabe; hard to keep himself from sinking into sullen bitterness. But he knew that he could keep his chin up—in a very positive way he knew this, and the knowledge renewed his strength. Clara and Blacky and he would be partners in developing the ranch. What more could he ask than to share their work? Some day Queen would drop another palomino filly and she would be his from the very beginning. Maybe not another Cloud, but, well . . .

The familiar rattling of the pickup came to his ear. Good! He had missed seeing Blacky.

Orrin looked up the hill. Mrs. Martin had come outside to meet the pickup. Blacky climbed out, followed by Barbara Johnson. Orrin was glad that she had come along, for he had wanted to talk to her, and it would be easier to do so with other people around.

The three came down the hill toward him, but if they were talking, their voices were too low to be heard. Orrin continued to brush Cloud until they entered the paddock. Then he looked up.

Barbara ran forward to see Cloud at close range, to feel the vitality of her warm, damp body. "Orrin," she cried huskily, "she hasn't a scratch on her. It's wonderful, isn't it?"

"Yes, it is."

"Charley told us you brought her back," Blacky said awkwardly to Orrin.

Orrin stepped away from Cloud. He had the feeling that he was surer of himself than any of the others. "This probably sounds crazy, but I'm going to sleep in the stable tonight. She'll know why after it's all over."

Clara looked back in the direction of the house, and Blacky cleared his throat. Barbara smiled, her eyes filled with understanding.

"I heard from Gabe's ranch," Orrin told Barbara quietly.

"Oh," Barbara exclaimed. "I was afraid it would be bad news. May I read the letter?"

Orrin drew it from his pocket and handed it to her. While she was doing this, he gave Cloud a few more swipes with the brush, and tried to rumple her damp mane.

"Orrin!" Barbara exclaimed. "Did you read the whole letter?"

"I guess I didn't."

"Listen!" The paper was shaking in her hands, and her voice had an excited quaver. "*You can tell Gabe he can draw his time after he gets back with that chestnut. He's plumb lazy. If he wasn't, he would have trained the filly himself instead of turning her over to my son to take care of. As far as that goes—*" Barbara tried to laugh, but for the moment her breath raced too fast to allow her to do so. "It's all here," she cried. "Gabe didn't raise that filly at all. Oh, Orrin—" She stopped suddenly and began to cry.

Orrin had thought he understood what Barbara was

saying, and a great feeling of elation spread over him. But when he saw her cry, it checked the feeling at once. He stood perplexed while Clara took the letter gently from Barbara and read it.

Orrin's hand made a helpless gesture toward Barbara. "Whatever it is, don't let it get you," he said.

The sobs suddenly stopped, but tears were still in Barbara's eyes, although she was smiling. "First time I ever did that," she said apologetically. "I thought that only women cried when they were happy."

Orrin heard Clara say, "Blacky, there's no doubt about it. Gabe tried to trick you by getting somebody else to train his filly. He doesn't deserve a single bit of the credit."

The rancher's leathery face grew darker, and the lines about his mouth hardened. "A promise is a promise," he said grimly. "Orrin, the palomino belongs to you now."

Orrin gasped. Things had moved so unexpectedly. He tried to whistle, but no audible sound came; yet Cloud thrust her head toward him and nickered. Orrin's hands slid hesitantly along the filly's neck, as if he were not yet sure she was really his. But he looked into her intelligent eyes with a proud grin that slowly broadened.

The other three were drawing quietly away. "Goodby," Barbara called to him.

" 'By. See you later," his gaze barely turning from Cloud. Suddenly an important thought came to him; he looked around in time to see the Martins entering the house.

"Wait here," he told Cloud, and sprinted up the hill.

Blacky and Clara were in the living room when Orrin ran through the kitchen and up the stairs. They looked at him in surprise as he came back with a package under his arm.

"For you," Orrin told Clara, holding out the package.

Clara Martin removed the wrapping and lifted the corner of the box to peek inside. "Why, Orrin!" she exclaimed. She looked into the box again. "It is, Orrin. It's a ruffly dress."

"Sure," Orrin grinned, "we're going to a party and celebrate."

Clara held the dress up in front of her. But she looked as if she too were going to cry.

Blacky coughed, and with eyebrows pulled fiercely toward his sharp black eyes, he began to study the rodeo picture on the wall.

Then Clara's serene expression returned. "You bought this when you thought we were losing Cloud. That was right fine of you, Orrin . . . But don't let us keep you from your filly, hear? Go on out to her."

"Do you mind?" Orrin said, but he was out of the house and running downhill almost before he had spoken the last word.

A few swift, buoyant strides and Orrin was alone with his palomino. He talked to her, and the words thrilled like an ageless song. The spirited filly tossed her head and uttered a whinny that was as unmistakable as a spoken invitation.

With a single leap Orrin sprang to her back and twisted his hands into her mane. Off Cloud dashed with her splendid head high and silvery tail billowing. Through the pasture gate and off through the field they raced, while Orrin bent down and felt her damp mane licking at his cheek.

A multitude of separate, tingling sensations stirred inside him, swelling together like gathering tributaries, and pouring themselves into one heaving torrent. Suddenly he opened his mouth and laughed as he had not laughed in years—laughed in the joy of the present and the years that lay ahead.

Cloud tilted one golden ear backward to catch the sound, and Orrin laughed again as he felt her answering burst of speed. His thoughts moved with the wild abandon of the pace until thoughts and hoofbeats merged into the one cadence: *We're together ... together ... together ... together ...*